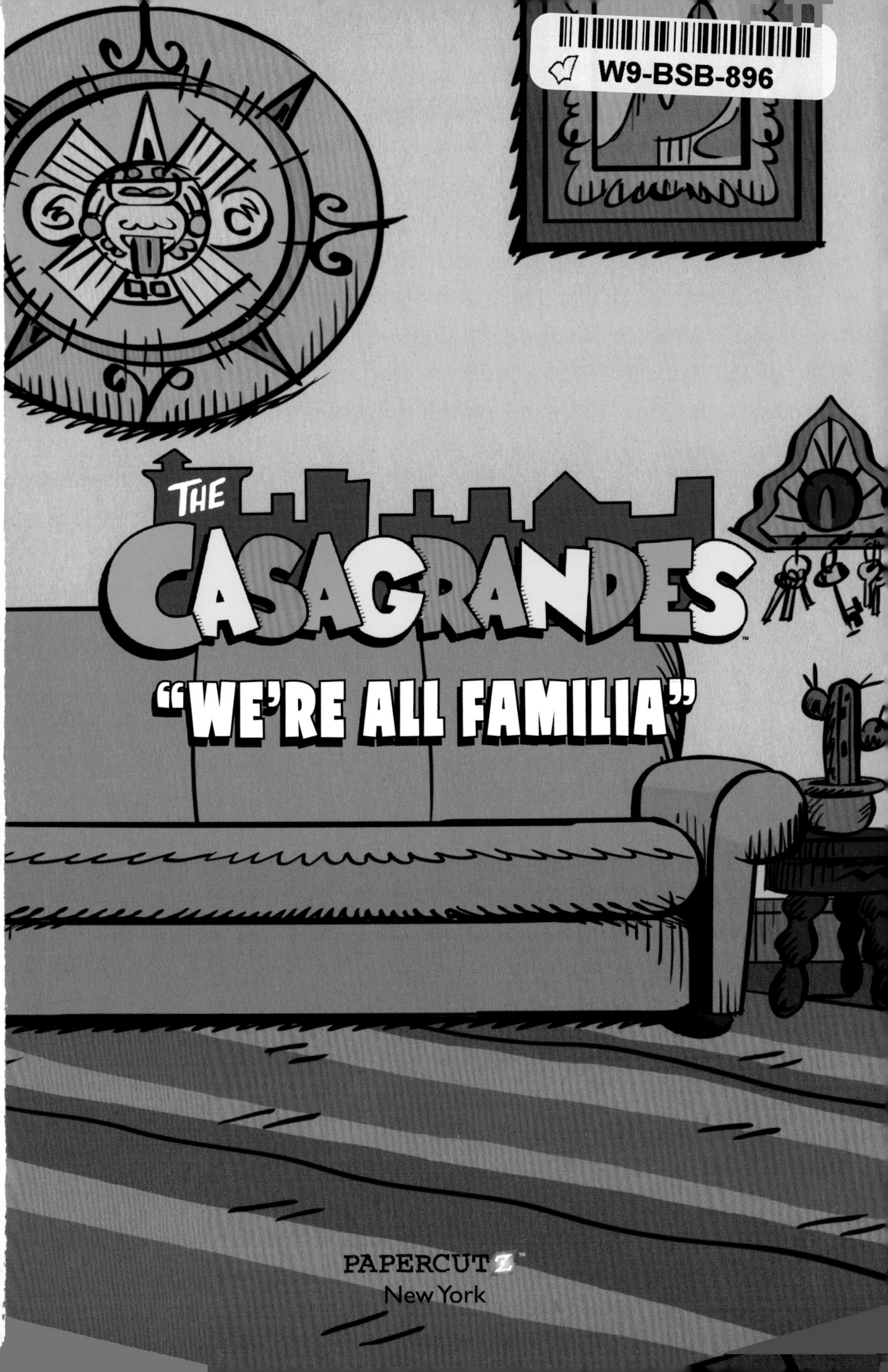

THE CASAGRANDES™

"WE'RE ALL FAMILIA"

PAPERCUTZ™
New York

nickelodeon GRAPHIC NOVELS AVAILABLE FROM PAPERCUTZ

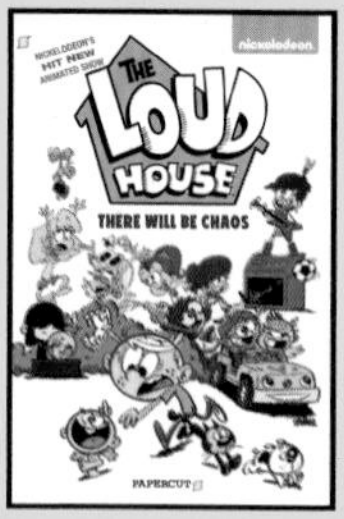
THE LOUD HOUSE
#1
"There Will Be Chaos"

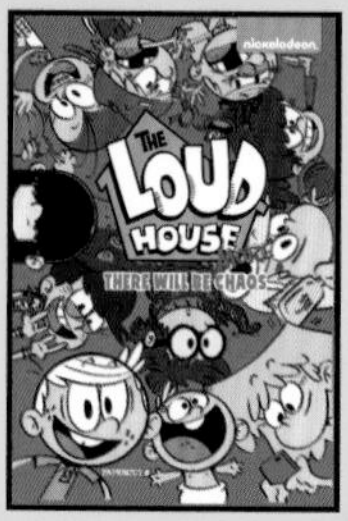
THE LOUD HOUSE
#2
"There Will Be More Chaos"

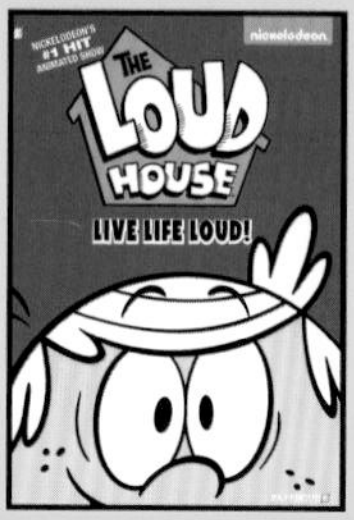
THE LOUD HOUSE
#3
"Live Life Loud!"

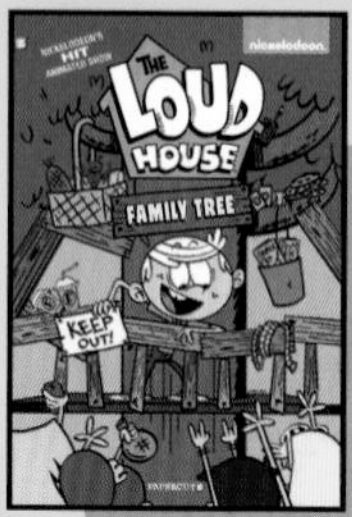
THE LOUD HOUSE
#4
"Family Tree"

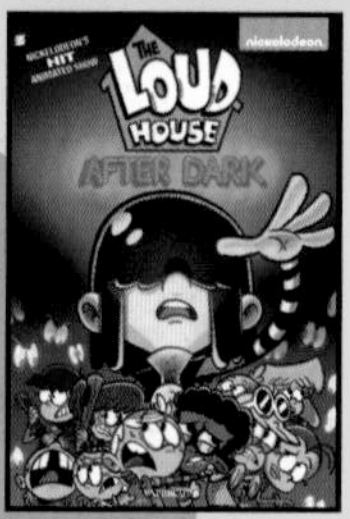
THE LOUD HOUSE
#5
"After Dark"

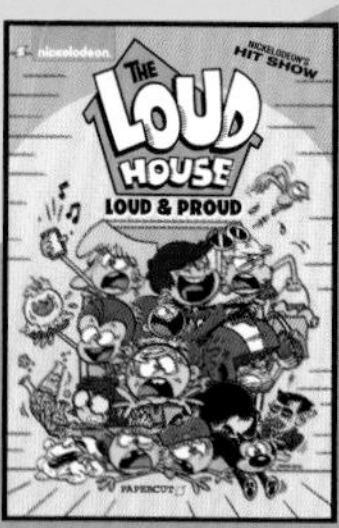
THE LOUD HOUSE
#6
"Loud and Proud"

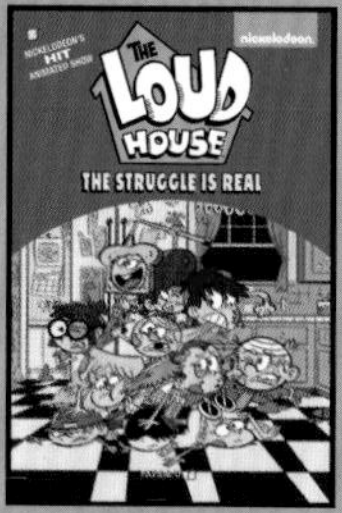
THE LOUD HOUSE
#7
"The Struggle is Real"

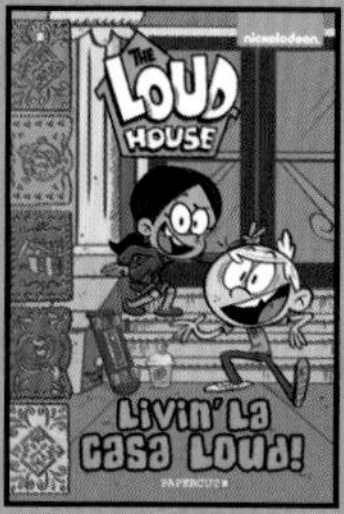
THE LOUD HOUSE
#8
"Livin' La Casa Loud"

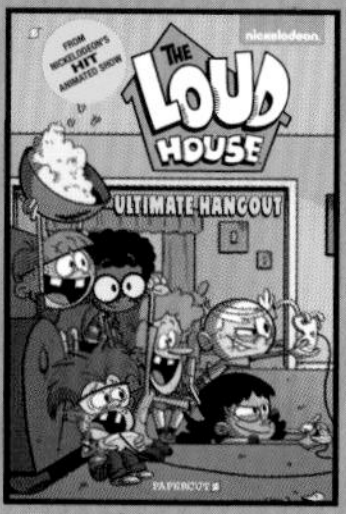
THE LOUD HOUSE
#9
"Ultimate Hangout"

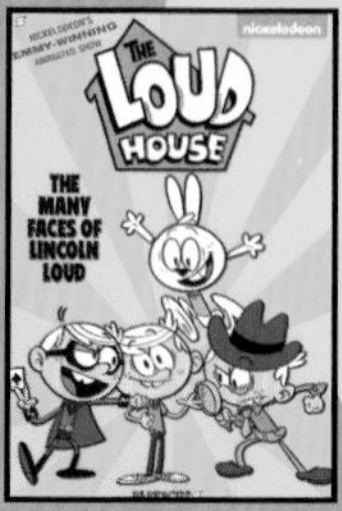
THE LOUD HOUSE
#10
"The Many Faces of Lincoln Loud"

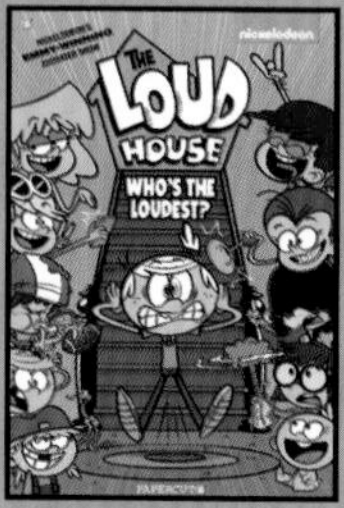
THE LOUD HOUSE
#11
"Who's the Loudest?"

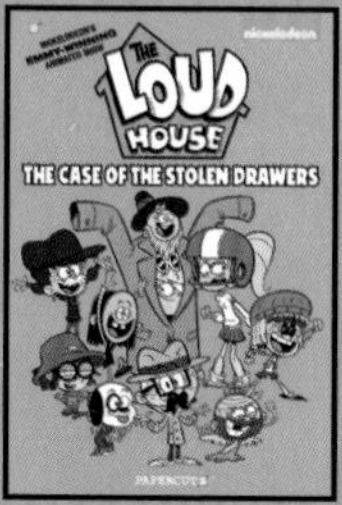
THE LOUD HOUSE
#12
"The Case of the Stolen Drawers"

COMING SOON

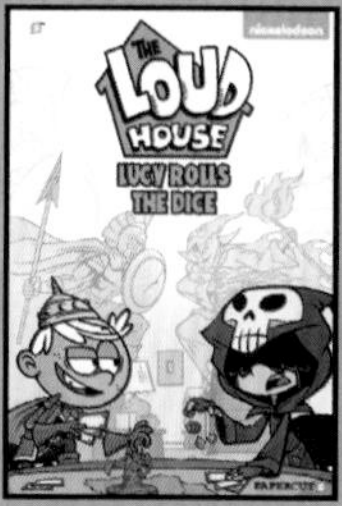
THE LOUD HOUSE
#13
"Lucy Rolls the Dice"

COMING SOON

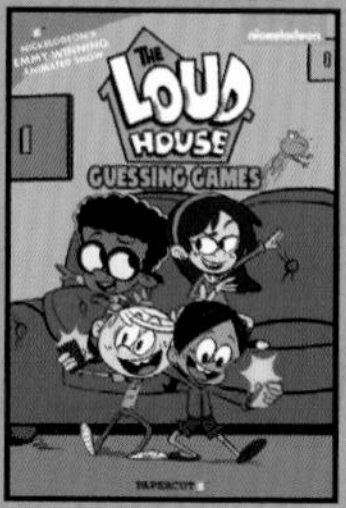
THE LOUD HOUSE
#14
"Guessing Games"

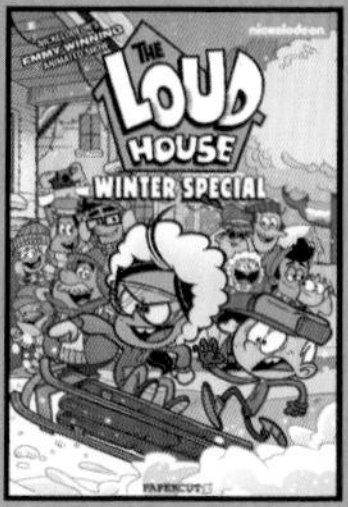
THE LOUD HOUSE
WINTER SPECIAL

COMING SOON

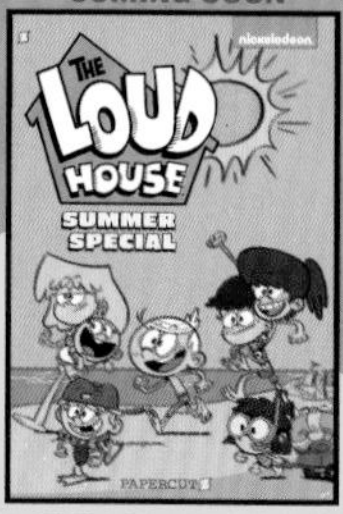
THE LOUD HOUSE
SUMMER SPECIAL

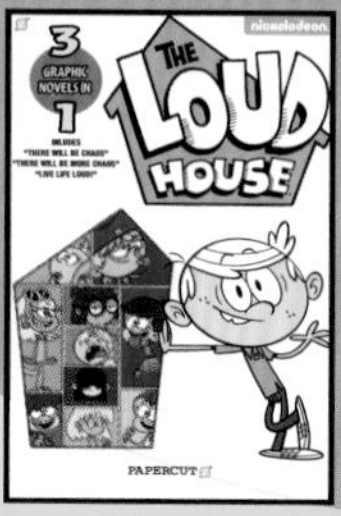
THE LOUD HOUSE
3 IN 1
#1

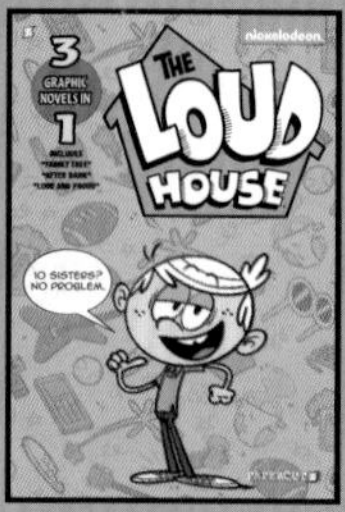
THE LOUD HOUSE
3 IN 1
#2

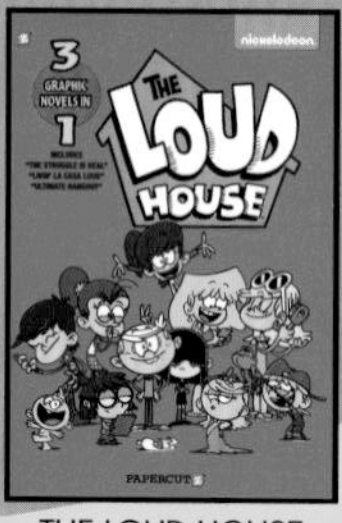
THE LOUD HOUSE
3 IN 1
#3

COMING SOON

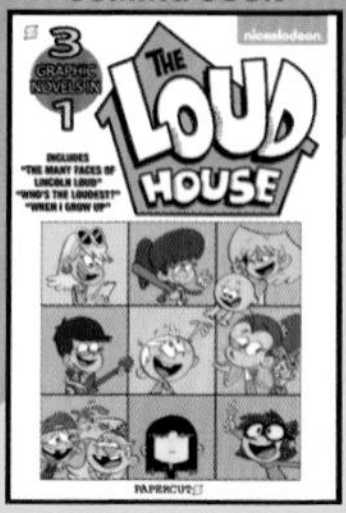
THE LOUD HOUSE
3 IN 1
#4

The Loud House and The Casagrandes graphic novels and specials are available for $7.99 each in paperback, $12.99 each in hardcover. THE LOUD HOUSE 3 IN 1 graphic novels are available for $14.99 each in paperback only. Available from booksellers everywhere. You can also order online from Papercutz.com, or call 1-800-886-1223, Monday through Friday, 9-5 EST. MC, Visa, and AmEx accepted. To order by mail, please add $5.00 for postage and handling for the first book ordered, $1.00 for each additional book and make check payable to NBM Publishing.
Send to: Papercutz, 160 Broadway, Suite 700, East Wing, New York, NY 10038.

THE CASAGRANDES

#1 "WE'RE ALL FAMILIA"

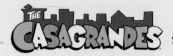

nickelodeon THE CASAGRANDES #1 "WE'RE ALL FAMILIA"

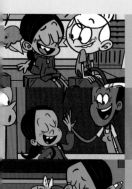

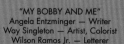

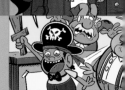

"RAIN, RAIN, HERE TO STAY"
Andrew Brooks — Writer
Erin Hyde — Artist, Colorist
Wilson Ramos Jr. — Letterer

"WORKED UP"
Sammie Crowley & Whitney Wetta — Writers
Ida Hem — Artist, Letterer
Hallie Lal — Colorist

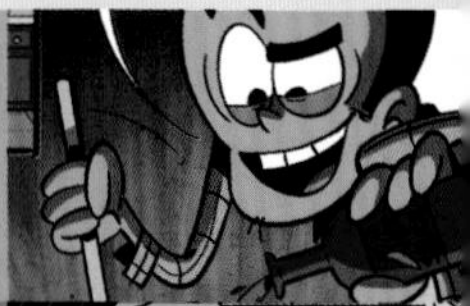

"MY BOBBY AND ME"
Angela Entzminger — Writer
Way Singleton — Artist, Colorist
Wilson Ramos Jr. — Letterer

"BABES IN THE CITY"
Sammie Crowley & Whitney Wetta — Writers
Ida Hem — Artist, Colorist, Letterer

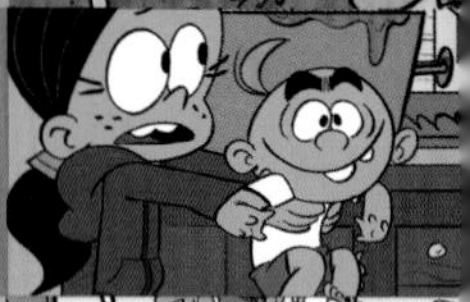

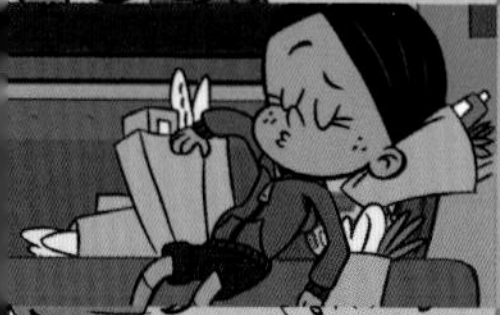

"SKATE FORCE GO!"
Rebecca E. Banks — Writer
Zazo Aguiar — Penciler, Inker, Colorist
Karolyne Rocha — Inker
Vic Miyuki — Colorist
Wilson Ramos Jr. — Letterer

"A PIRATE'S LIFE FOR CJ"
Whitney Wetta — Writer
Jared Morgan — Artist, Colorist, Letterer

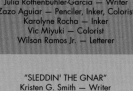

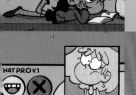

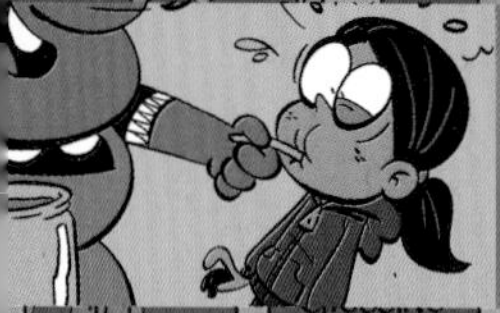

"TOUGH HOOKY"
Jared Morgan
Writer, Artist, Colorist, Letterer

"ROCK-A-BYE, CARLITOS"
Julia Rothenbuhler-Garcia — Writer
Zazo Aguiar — Penciler, Inker, Colorist
Karolyne Rocha — Inker
Vic Miyuki — Colorist
Wilson Ramos Jr. — Letterer

CARLITOS

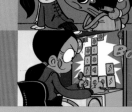

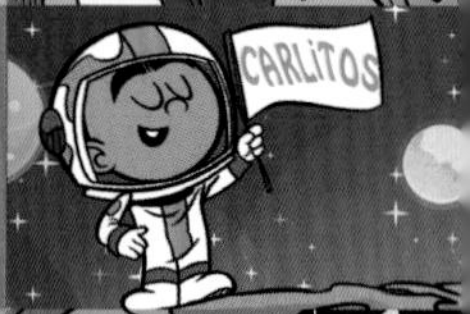

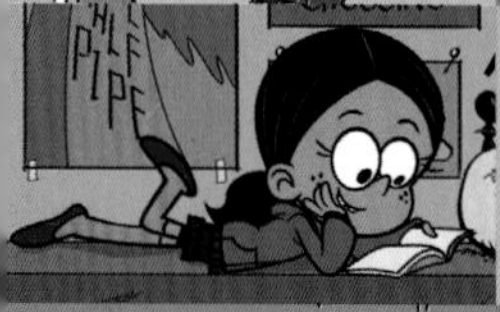

"GREAT ESCAPE"
Derek Fridolfs — Writer
Suzannah Rowntree— Penciler
Zazo Aguiar — Inker, Colorist
Wilson Ramos Jr. — Letterer

"SLEDDIN' THE GNAR"
Kristen G. Smith — Writer
Ron Bradley — Artist, Colorist
Wilson Ramos Jr. — Letterer

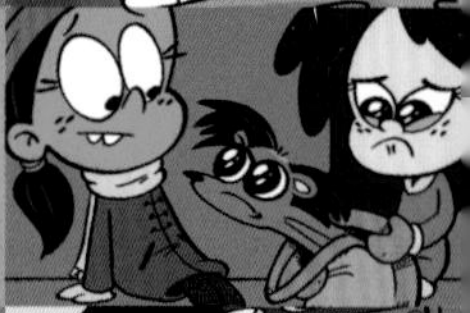

"MAYBE IT'S NATURAL"
Jared Morgan
Writer, Artist, Colorist, Letterer

"FOR A FEW TICKETS MORE"
Jair Holguin — Writer
Erin Hyde — Artist, Colorist
Wilson Ramos Jr. — Letterer

MAAIKE SCHERFF and CAUE ZUNCHINI — Cover Artists
JAMES SALERNO — Sr. Art Director/Nickelodeon
JAYJAY JACKSON — Design
KEVIN SULLIVAN, KRISTEN G. SMITH, PRINCESS BIZARES, DANA CLUVERIUS, MOLLIE FREILICH, NEIL WADE, MIGUEL PUGA, LALO ALCARAZ, and IZABELLA ALVAREZ — Special Thanks
JEFF WHITMAN — Editor
JOAN HILTY — Editor/Nickelodeon
JIM SALICRUP
Editor-in-Chief

ISBN: 978-1-5458-0623-4 paperback edition
ISBN: 978-1-5458-0622-7 hardcover edition

www.papercutz.com

Papercutz books may be purchased for business or promotional use. For information on bulk purchases please contact Macmillan Corporate and Premium Sales Department at (800) 221-7945 x5442.

Printed in Turkey
April 2022

Distributed by Macmillan
Second Printing

THE CASAGRANDES

Theme Song Performed by: ALLY BROOKE
Theme Song Composed by: GERMAINE FRANCO
Lyrics by: GERMAINE FRANCO, MIKE RUBINER & LALO ALCARAZ
Rap Lyrics Performed by: IZABELLA ALVAREZ

I'm in the big city with my big familia [family]

Everyday here is my favorite día [day]

One big house and our family store
Food and laughter ¡y mucho amor! [and a lot of
love!]

Tíos [aunts and uncles], abuelos [grandparents],
all of my primos [cousins]...

A dog, a parrot, amigos! [friends!]

We're one big family now!
Sundays and Mondays
They're all fun days when you're with the...
Casagrandes!
¡Mucha vida! [A lot of life!]

Casagrandes!
¡Bienvenida! [Welcome!]

Casagrandes!
¡Mucha risa! [A lot of laughs!]

Casagrandes!
We're all familia! [Family!]

¡Tan-tan! [Tah-dah!]

MEET THE CASAGRANDES *and friends!*

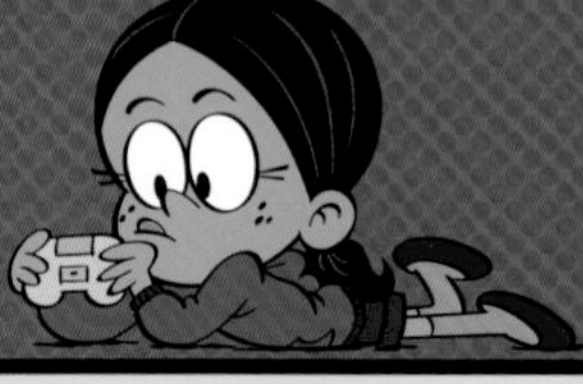

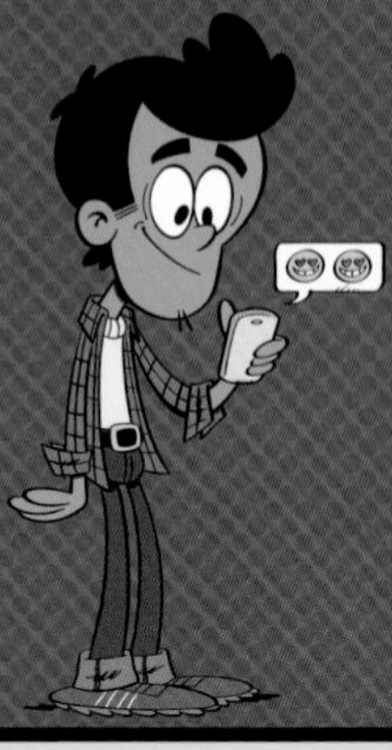

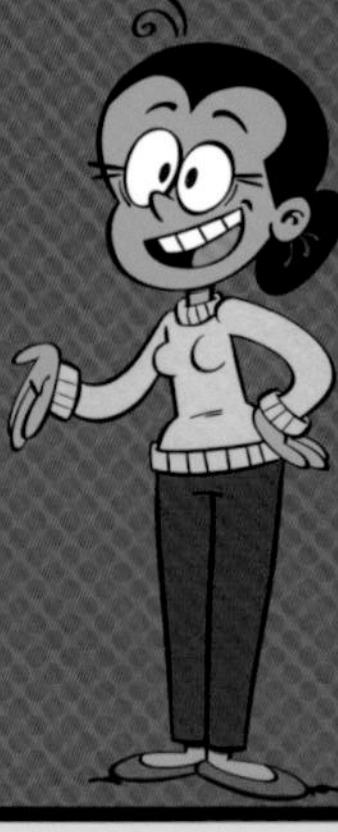

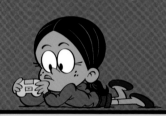

RONNIE ANNE SANTIAGO

Ronnie Anne's a skateboarding city girl now. She's fearless, free-spirited, and always quick to come up with a plan. She's one tough cookie, but she also has a sweet side. Ronnie Anne loves helping her family, and that's taught her to help others, too. When she's not pitching in at the family *mercado*, you can find her exploring the neighborhood with her best friend Sid, or ordering hot dogs with her skater buds Casey, Nikki, and Sameer. Having a family as big as the Casagrandes has taught Ronnie Anne to deal with anything life throws her way.

BOBBY SANTIAGO

Bobby is Ronnie Anne's big bro. He's a student and one of the hardest workers in the city. He loves his family and loves working at the *mercado*. As his abuelo's right hand man, Bobby can't wait to take over the family business one day. He's a big kid at heart, and his clumsiness gets him into some sticky situations at work, like locking himself in the freezer. Mercado mishaps aside, everyone in the neighborhood loves to come to the store and talk to Bobby.

MARIA CASAGRANDE SANTIAGO

Maria is Bobby and Ronnie Anne's mom. As a nurse at the city hospital, she's hardworking and even harder to gross out. For years, Maria, Bobby, and Ronnie Anne were used to only having each other… but now that they've moved in with their Casagrande relatives, they're embracing big family life. Maria is the voice of reason in the household and known for her always-on-the-go attitude. Her long work hours means she doesn't always get to spend time with Bobby and Ronnie Anne; but when she does, she makes that time count.

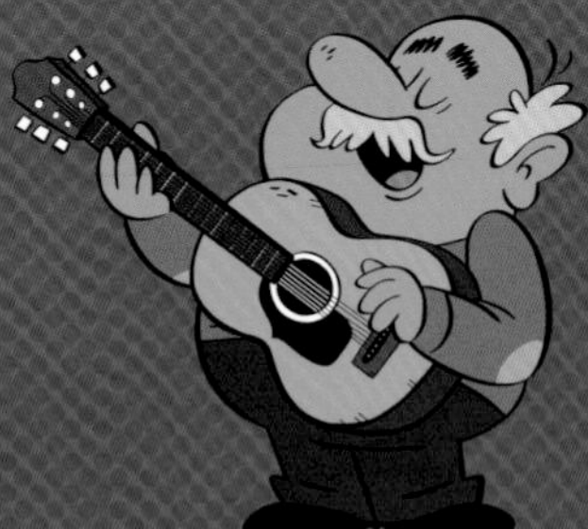

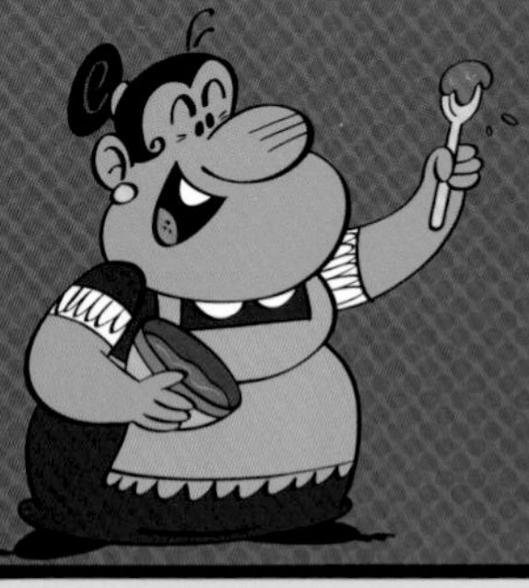

HECTOR CASAGRANDE

Hector is Carlos and Maria's dad, and the *abuelo* of the family (that means grandpa)! He owns the *mercado* on the ground floor of their apartment building and takes great pride in his work, his family, and being the unofficial "mayor" of the block. He loves to tell stories, share his ideas, and gossip (even though he won't admit to it). You can find him working in the *mercado*, playing guitar, or watching his favorite *telenovela*.

ROSA CASAGRANDE

Rosa is Carlos and Maria's mom and the *abuela* of the family (that means grandma)! She's the head of the household, the wisest Casagrande, and the master cook with a superhuman ability to tell when anyone in the house is hungry. She often tries to fix problems or illnesses with traditional Mexican home remedies and potions. She's very protective of her family… sometimes a little too much.

CARLOS CASAGRANDE

Carlos is Maria's brother. He's married to Frida, and together they have four kids: Carlota, C.J., Carl, and Carlitos. Carlos is a Professor of Cultural Studies at a local college. Usually he has his heads in the clouds or his nose in a textbook. Relatively easygoing, Carlos is a loving father and an enthusiastic teacher who tries to get his kids interested in their Mexican heritage.

FRIDA PUGA CASAGRANDE

Frida is Carlos, C.J., Carl, and Carlitos' mom. She's an art professor and a performance artist, and is always looking for new ways to express herself. She's got a big heart and isn't shy about her emotions. Frida tends to cry when she's sad, happy, angry, or any other emotion you can think of. She's always up for fun, is passionate about her art, and loves her family more than anything.

CARLOTA CASAGRANDE

Carlota is CJ, Carl, and Carlitos' older sister. A social media influencer, she's excited to be like a big sister to Ronnie Anne. She's a force to be reckoned with, and is always trying to share her distinctive vintage style tips with Ronnie Anne.

CARLITOS CASAGRANDE

Carlitos is the baby of the family, and is always copying the behavior of everyone in the household—even if they aren't human. He's a playful and silly baby who loves to play with the family pets.

CJ (CARLOS JR.) CASAGRANDE

CJ is Carlota's younger brother and Carl and Carlitos' older brother. He was born with Down Syndrome. He lights up any room with his infectious smile and is always ready to play. He's obsessed with pirates and is BFFs with Bobby. He likes to wear a bowtie to any family occasion, and you can always catch him laughing or helping his *abuela*.

CARL CASAGRANDE

Carl is wise beyond his years. He's confident, outgoing, and puts a lot of time and effort into looking good. He likes to think of himself as a suave businessman and doesn't like to get caught playing with his action figures or wearing his footie PJs. Even though Bobby is nothing but nice to him, Carl sees his big cousin as his biggest rival.

LALO

Lalo is a slobbery bull mastiff who thinks he's a lapdog. He's not the smartest pup, and gets scared easily… but he loves his family and loves to cuddle.

SERGIO

Sergio is the Casagrandes' beloved pet parrot. He's a blunt, sassy bird who "thinks" he's full of wisdom and always has something to say. The Casagrandes have to keep a close eye on their credit card as Sergio is addicted to online shopping and is always asking the family to buy him some new gadget he saw on TV. Sergio is most loyal to Rosa and serves as her wing-man, partner-in-crime, taste-tester, and confidant. Sergio is quite popular in the neighborhood and is always up for a good time. When he's not working part time at the *mercado* (aka messing with Bobby), he can be found hanging with his roommate Ronnie Anne, partying with Sancho and his other pigeon pals, or trying to get his ex-girlfriend, Priscilla (an ostrich at the zoo), to respond to him.

SID CHANG

Sid is Ronnie Anne's quirky best friend. She's new to the city but dives headfirst into everything she finds interesting. She and her family just moved into the apartment one floor above the Casagrandes. In fact, Sid's bedroom is right above Ronnie Anne's. A dream come true for any BFFs.

CASEY

Casey is a happy-go-lucky kid who's always there to help. He knows all the best spots to get grub in Great Lakes City. When he is not skateboarding with the crew, he loves working with his dad, Alberto, on their Cubano sandwich food truck.

SAMEER

Sameer is a goofy sweetheart who wishes he was taller, but what he lacks in height, he makes up for with his impressive hair and sweet skate moves. He is always down for the unexpected adventure and loves entertaining his friends with his spooky tales!

NIKKI

Nikki is as daring as she is easygoing and laughs when she is nervous. When she's not hanging with her buds at the skatepark, she likes checking out the newest sneakers and reading books about the paranormal.

LAIRD

Laird is a total team player and the newest member of Ronnie Anne's friends. Despite often being on the wrong end of misfortune, Laird is an awesome skateboarder who can do tons of tricks...unfortunately stopping is not one of them.

STANLEY CHANG

Stanley Chang is Sid's dad. He's a conductor on the GLART-train that runs through the city. He's a patient man who likes to do Tai Chi when he gets stressed out. He likes to cheer up train commuters with fun facts, but emotionally he breaks down more than the train does.

BECCA CHANG

Becca Chang is Sid's mom. Like her daughter, Becca is quirky, smart, and funny. She works at the Great Lakes City Zoo and often brings her work home with her, which means the Chang household can also be a bit of a zoo.

ADELAIDE CHANG

Adelaide Chang is Sid's little sister. She's 6 years old, and has a flair for the dramatic. You can always find her trying to make her way into her big sister Sid's adventures.

LINCOLN LOUD

Lincoln is Ronnie Anne's dearest friend from Royal Woods. They still keep in touch and visit one another as often as they can. He has learned that surviving the Loud household with ten sisters means staying a step ahead. He's the man with a plan, always coming up with a way to get what he wants or deal with a problem, even if things inevitably go wrong. Lincoln's sisters may drive him crazy, but he loves them and is always willing to help out if they need him.

CLYDE McBRIDE

Clyde is Lincoln's partner in crime. He's always willing to go along with Lincoln's crazy schemes (even if he sees the flaws in them up-front). Lincoln and Clyde are two peas in a pod and share pretty much all of the same tastes in movies, comics, TV shows, toys — you name it. As an only child, Clyde envies Lincoln — how cool would it be to always have siblings around to talk to? But since Clyde spends so much time at the Loud household, he's almost an honorary sibling anyway.

ZACH GURDLE

Zach is a self-admitted nerd who's obsessed with aliens and conspiracy theories. He lives between a freeway and a circus, so the chaos of the Loud House doesn't faze him. He and Rusty occasionally butt heads, but deep down, it's all love.

STELLA

Stella is a quirky, carefree girl who's new to Royal Woods. She has tons of interests, like trying on wigs, playing laser tag, eating curly fries, and hanging with her friends. But what she loves the most is tech — she always wants to dismantle electronics and put them back together again.

"RAIN, RAIN, HERE TO STAY"

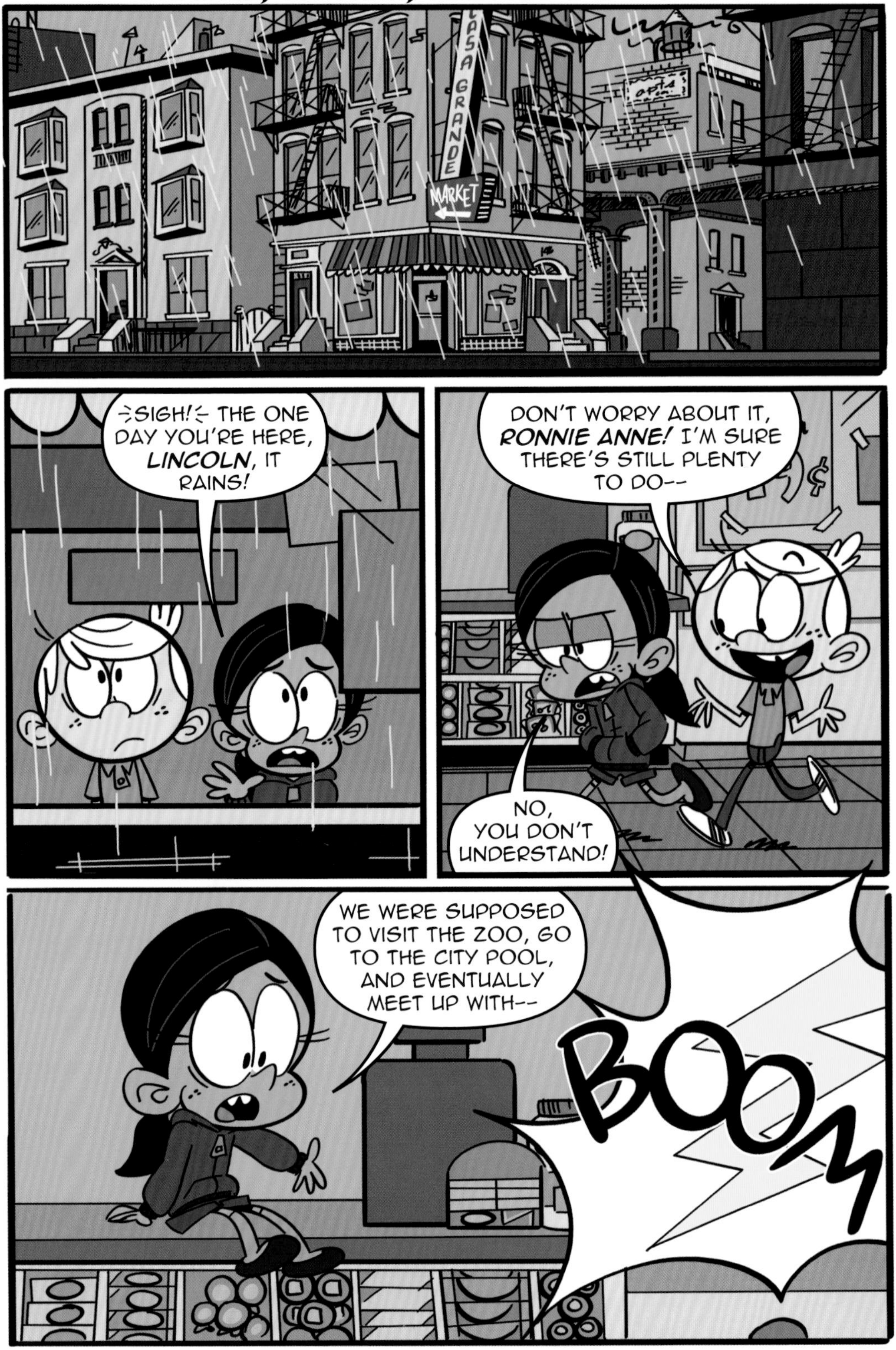
CASA GRANDE
MARKET
SIGH! THE ONE DAY YOU'RE HERE, **LINCOLN**, IT RAINS!
DON'T WORRY ABOUT IT, **RONNIE ANNE!** I'M SURE THERE'S STILL PLENTY TO DO--
NO, YOU DON'T UNDERSTAND!
WE WERE SUPPOSED TO VISIT THE ZOO, GO TO THE CITY POOL, AND EVENTUALLY MEET UP WITH--
BOOM

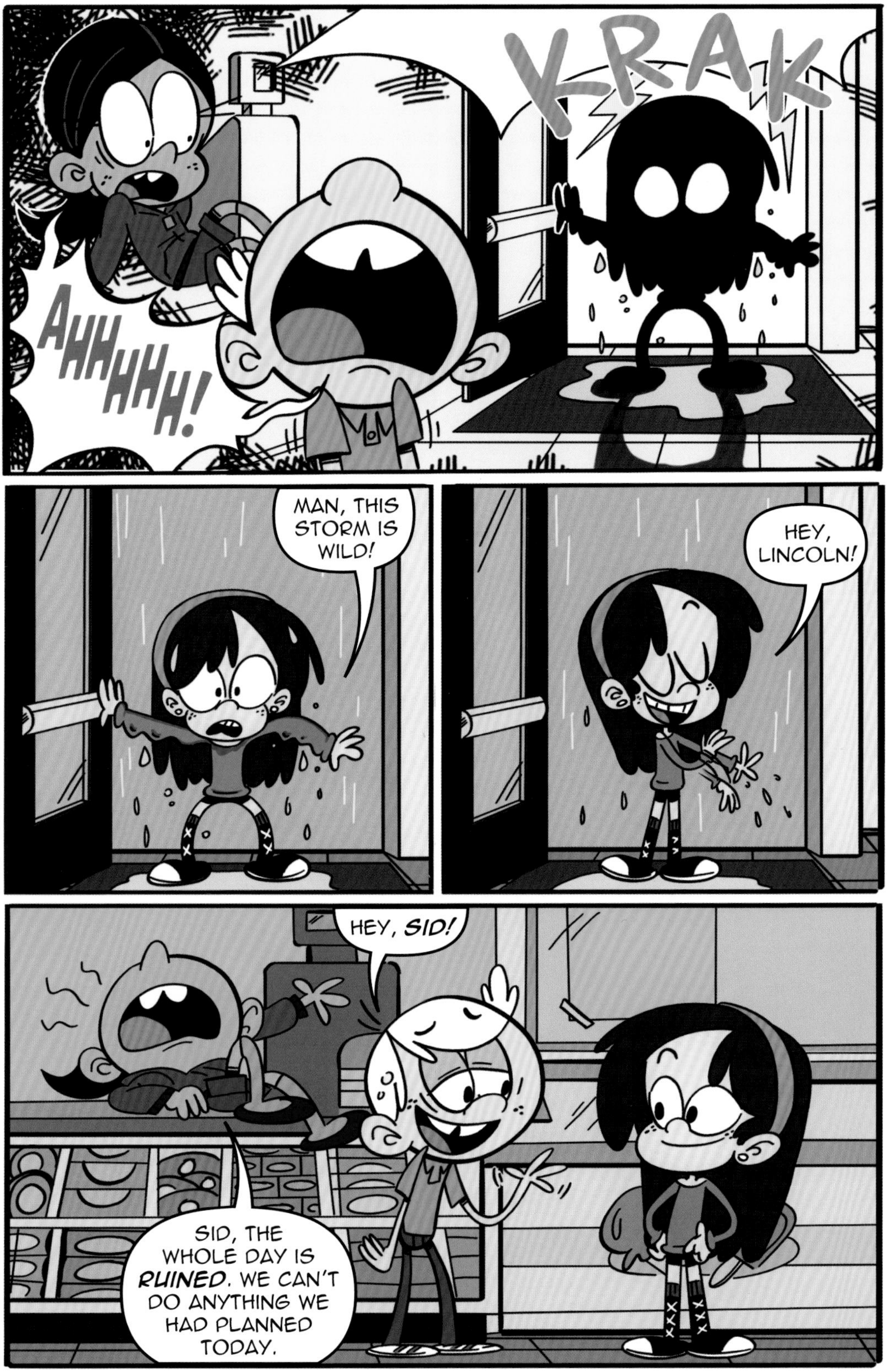
KRAK
AHHHHHH!
MAN, THIS STORM IS WILD!
HEY, LINCOLN!
HEY, SID!
SID, THE WHOLE DAY IS RUINED. WE CAN'T DO ANYTHING WE HAD PLANNED TODAY.

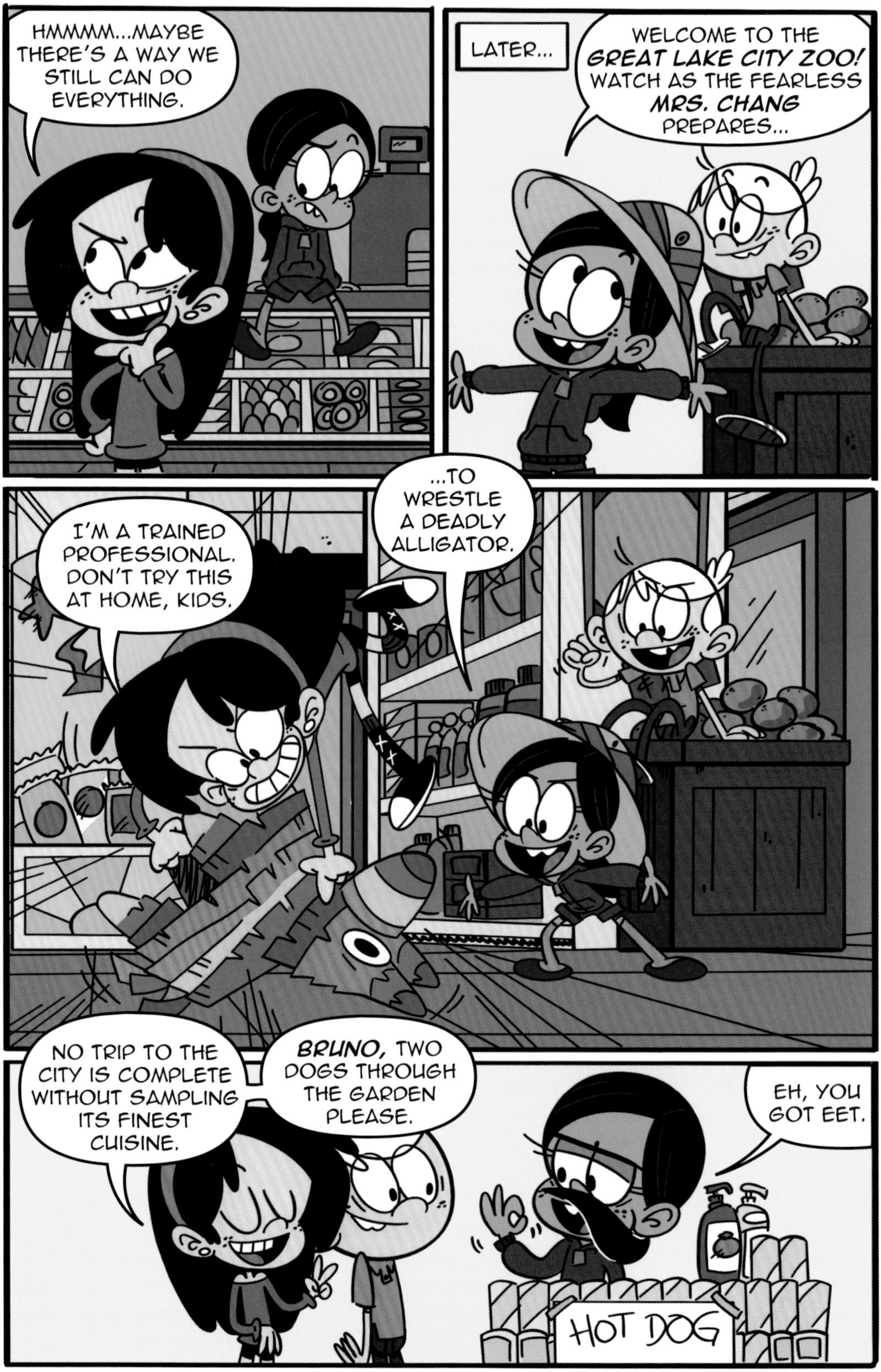
HMMMM...MAYBE THERE'S A WAY WE STILL CAN DO EVERYTHING.
LATER...
WELCOME TO THE GREAT LAKE CITY ZOO! WATCH AS THE FEARLESS MRS. CHANG PREPARES...
I'M A TRAINED PROFESSIONAL. DON'T TRY THIS AT HOME, KIDS.
...TO WRESTLE A DEADLY ALLIGATOR.
NO TRIP TO THE CITY IS COMPLETE WITHOUT SAMPLING ITS FINEST CUISINE.
BRUNO, TWO DOGS THROUGH THE GARDEN PLEASE.
EH, YOU GOT EET.
HOT DOG

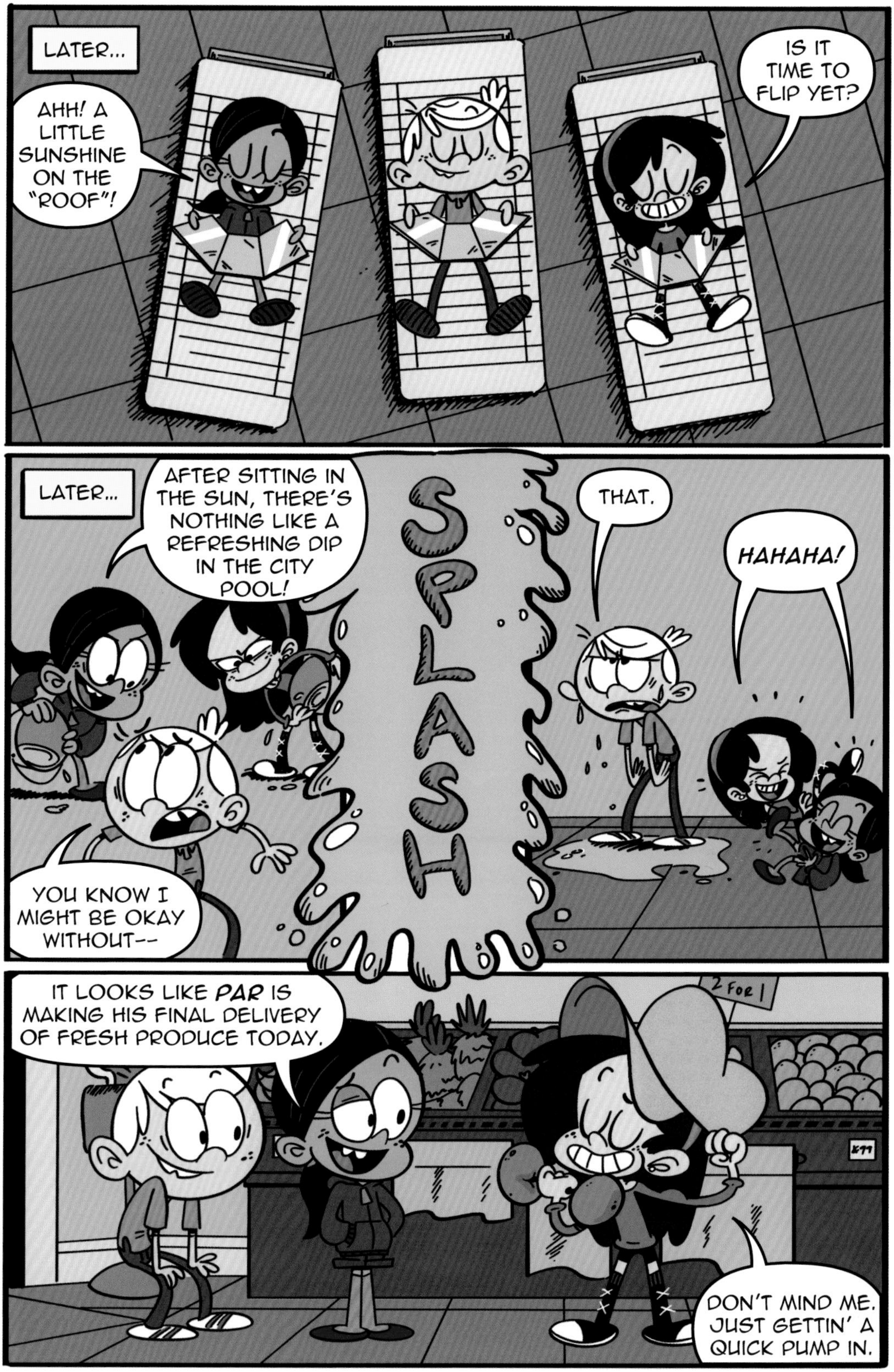
LATER...
AHH! A LITTLE SUNSHINE ON THE "ROOF"!
IS IT TIME TO FLIP YET?
LATER...
AFTER SITTING IN THE SUN, THERE'S NOTHING LIKE A REFRESHING DIP IN THE CITY POOL!
YOU KNOW I MIGHT BE OKAY WITHOUT--
SPLASH
THAT.
HAHAHA!
IT LOOKS LIKE *PAR* IS MAKING HIS FINAL DELIVERY OF FRESH PRODUCE TODAY.
2 FOR 1
DON'T MIND ME. JUST GETTIN' A QUICK PUMP IN.

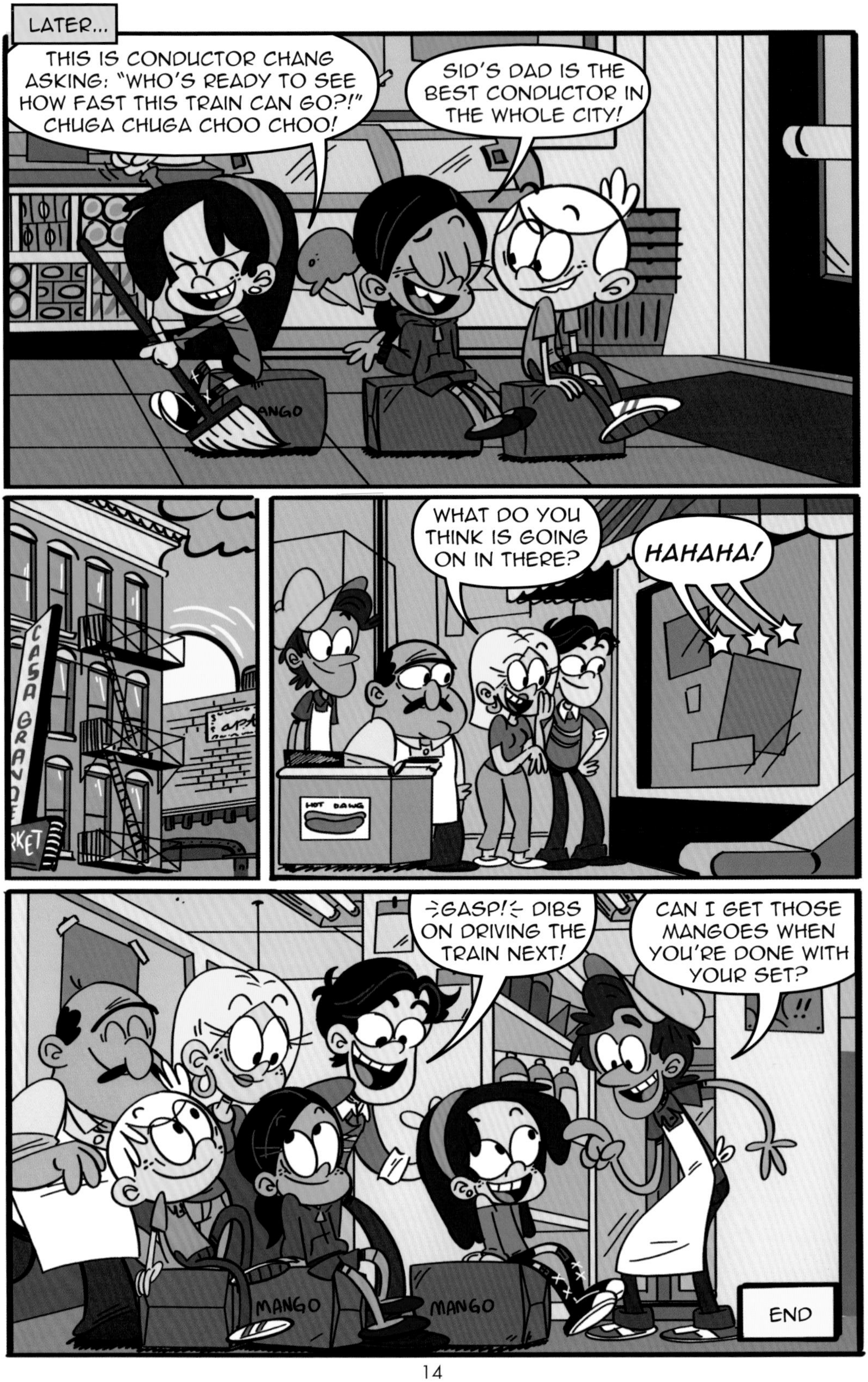
LATER...
THIS IS CONDUCTOR CHANG ASKING: "WHO'S READY TO SEE HOW FAST THIS TRAIN CAN GO?!" CHUGA CHUGA CHOO CHOO!
SID'S DAD IS THE BEST CONDUCTOR IN THE WHOLE CITY!
MANGO
CASA GRANDE
RKET
WHAT DO YOU THINK IS GOING ON IN THERE?
HAHAHA!
HOT DAWG
-GASP!- DIBS ON DRIVING THE TRAIN NEXT!
CAN I GET THOSE MANGOES WHEN YOU'RE DONE WITH YOUR SET?
MANGO
MANGO
END

"MY BOBBY AND ME"

GOOD MORNING, **BOBBY!** HAVE A GREAT DAY AT THE MERCADO.

ACTUALLY, I TOOK THE DAY OFF, **RONNIE ANNE.** WANTED TO SPEND SOME QUALITY TIME WITH MY FAVORITE LITTLE SISTER.

BOBBY, THAT'S SO **COOL!** YOU **NEVER** TAKE SATURDAY OFF.

FIGURED WE SHOULD EXPLORE THIS AMAZING CITY TOGETHER, **NINI.** I'VE GOT THE WHOLE DAY PLANNED!

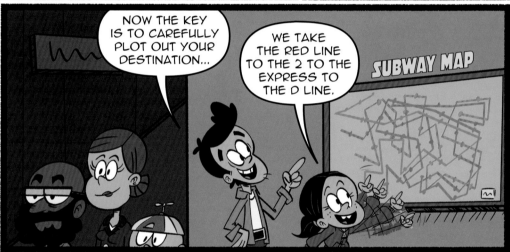

NOW THE KEY IS TO CAREFULLY PLOT OUT YOUR DESTINATION...

WE TAKE THE RED LINE TO THE 2 TO THE EXPRESS TO THE D LINE.

SUBWAY MAP

SO THE CITY PARK IS MY ALL-TIME FAVORITE PLACE TO UNWIND. YOU CAN FEED THE DUCKS, PLAY CHECKERS--

QUACK QUACK

AND **SHRED!** COME ON, BOBBY! I'LL SHOW YOU THE HALF PIPE.

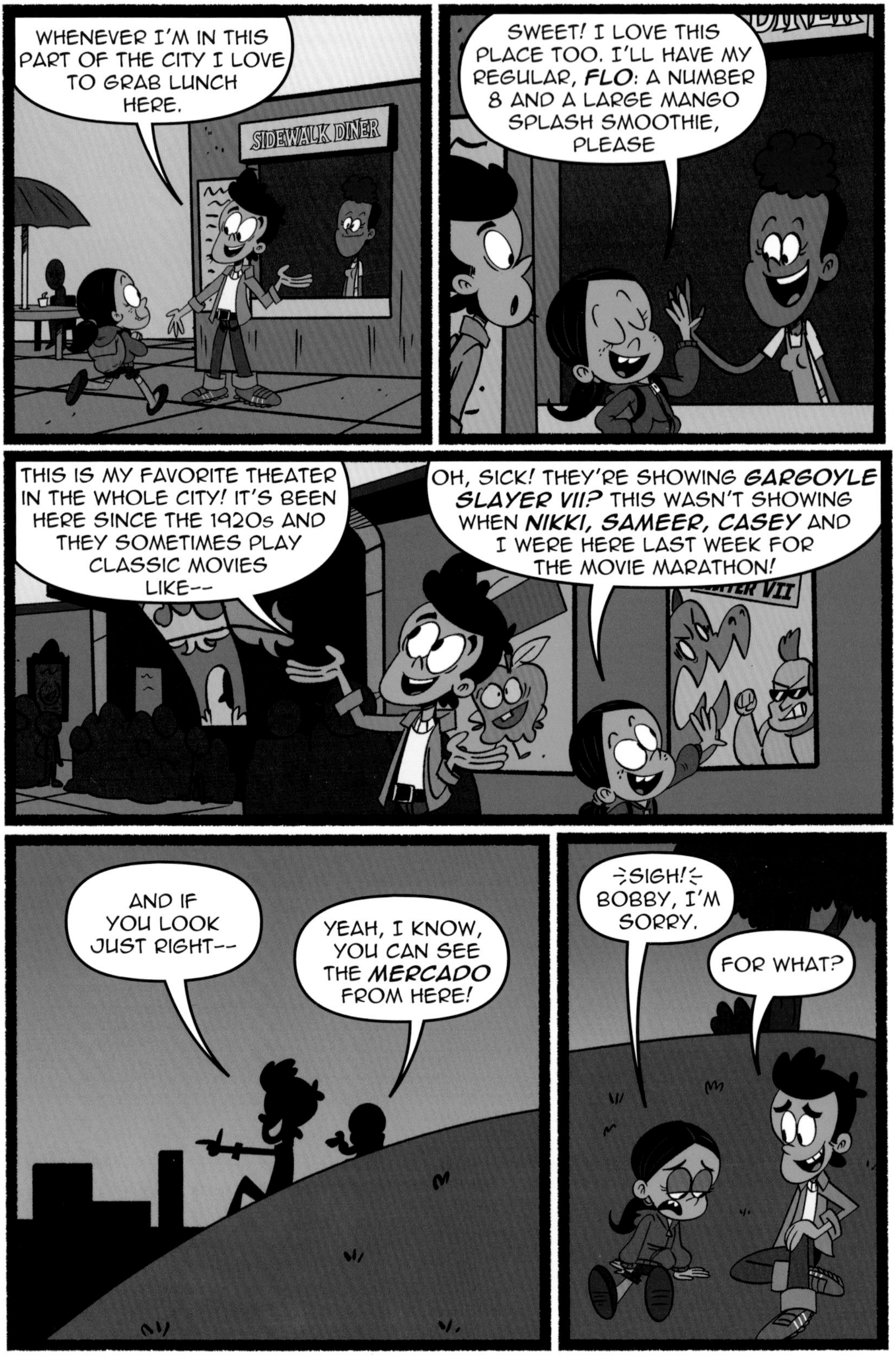
WHENEVER I'M IN THIS PART OF THE CITY I LOVE TO GRAB LUNCH HERE.
SIDEWALK DINER
SWEET! I LOVE THIS PLACE TOO. I'LL HAVE MY REGULAR, **FLO**: A NUMBER 8 AND A LARGE MANGO SPLASH SMOOTHIE, PLEASE
THIS IS MY FAVORITE THEATER IN THE WHOLE CITY! IT'S BEEN HERE SINCE THE 1920s AND THEY SOMETIMES PLAY CLASSIC MOVIES LIKE--
OH, SICK! THEY'RE SHOWING ***GARGOYLE SLAYER VII?*** THIS WASN'T SHOWING WHEN ***NIKKI, SAMEER, CASEY*** AND I WERE HERE LAST WEEK FOR THE MOVIE MARATHON!
AND IF YOU LOOK JUST RIGHT--
YEAH, I KNOW, YOU CAN SEE THE ***MERCADO*** FROM HERE!
SIGH! BOBBY, I'M SORRY.
FOR WHAT?

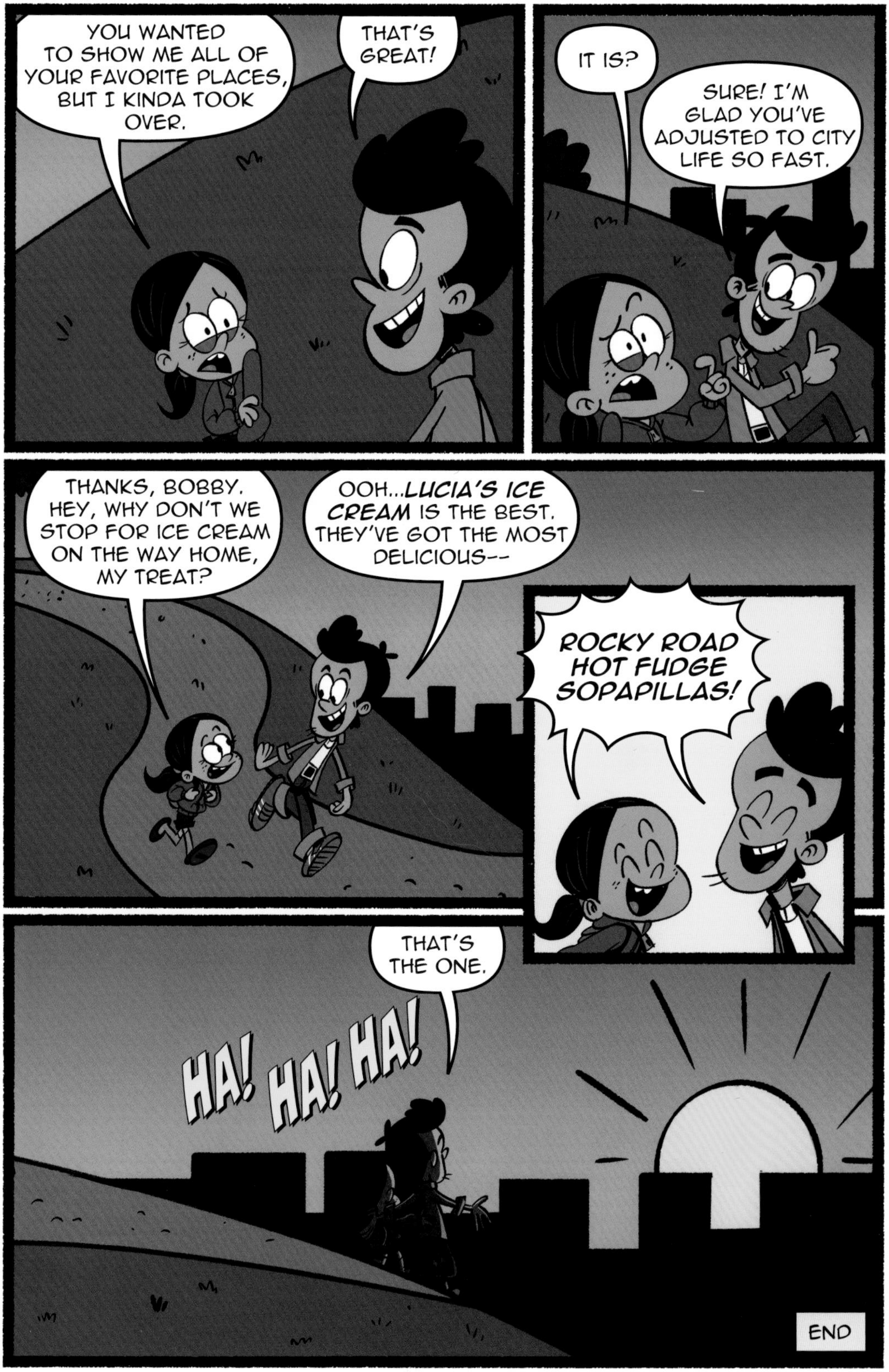
YOU WANTED TO SHOW ME ALL OF YOUR FAVORITE PLACES, BUT I KINDA TOOK OVER.
THAT'S GREAT!
IT IS?
SURE! I'M GLAD YOU'VE ADJUSTED TO CITY LIFE SO FAST.
THANKS, BOBBY. HEY, WHY DON'T WE STOP FOR ICE CREAM ON THE WAY HOME, MY TREAT?
OOH...*LUCIA'S ICE CREAM* IS THE BEST. THEY'VE GOT THE MOST DELICIOUS--
ROCKY ROAD HOT FUDGE SOPAPILLAS!
THAT'S THE ONE.
HA! HA! HA!
END

"SKATE FORCE GO!"

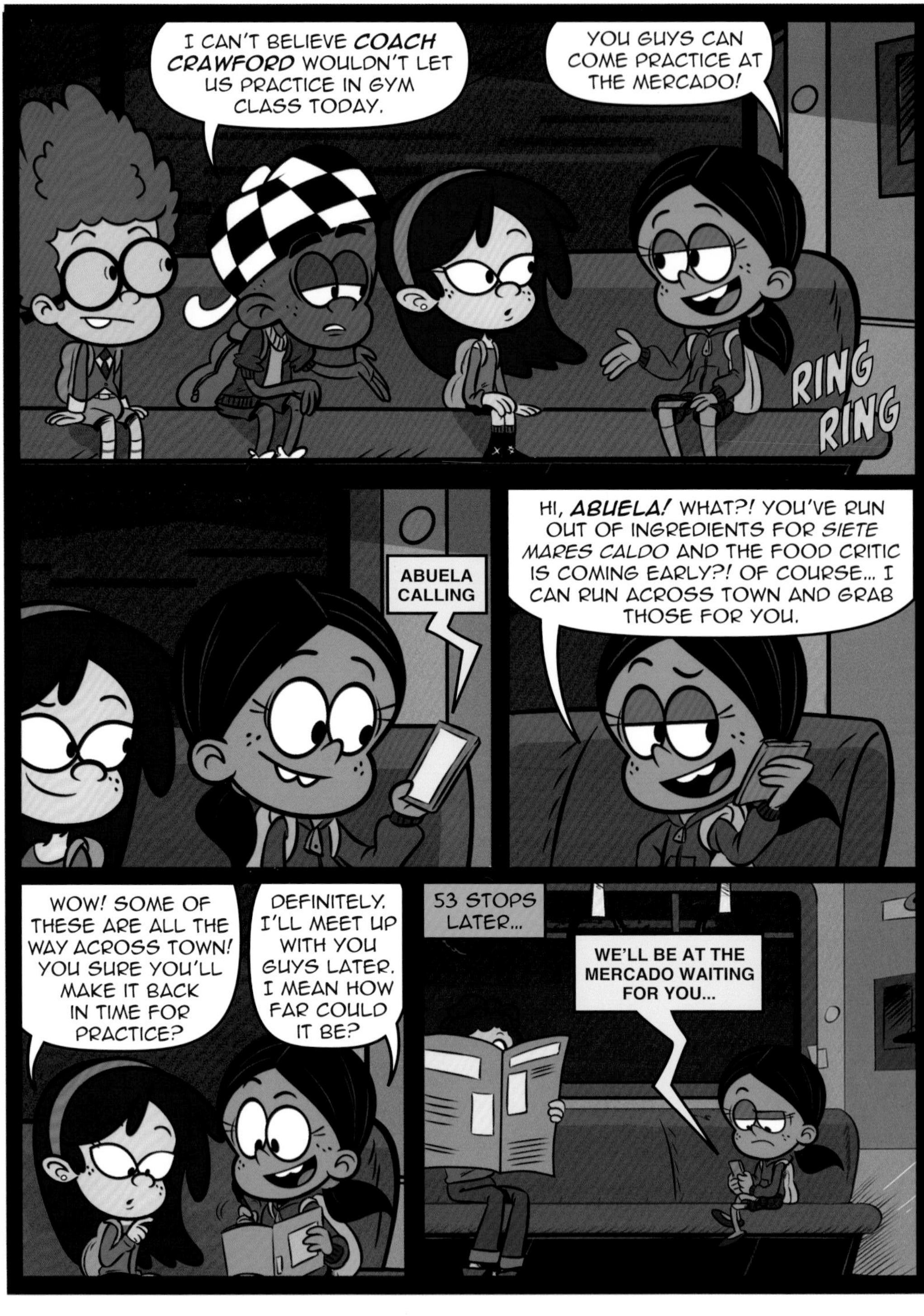
I CAN'T BELIEVE *COACH CRAWFORD* WOULDN'T LET US PRACTICE IN GYM CLASS TODAY.
YOU GUYS CAN COME PRACTICE AT THE MERCADO!
RING RING
ABUELA CALLING
HI, *ABUELA!* WHAT?! YOU'VE RUN OUT OF INGREDIENTS FOR *SIETE MARES CALDO* AND THE FOOD CRITIC IS COMING EARLY?! OF COURSE... I CAN RUN ACROSS TOWN AND GRAB THOSE FOR YOU.
WOW! SOME OF THESE ARE ALL THE WAY ACROSS TOWN! YOU SURE YOU'LL MAKE IT BACK IN TIME FOR PRACTICE?
DEFINITELY. I'LL MEET UP WITH YOU GUYS LATER. I MEAN HOW FAR COULD IT BE?
53 STOPS LATER...
WE'LL BE AT THE MERCADO WAITING FOR YOU...

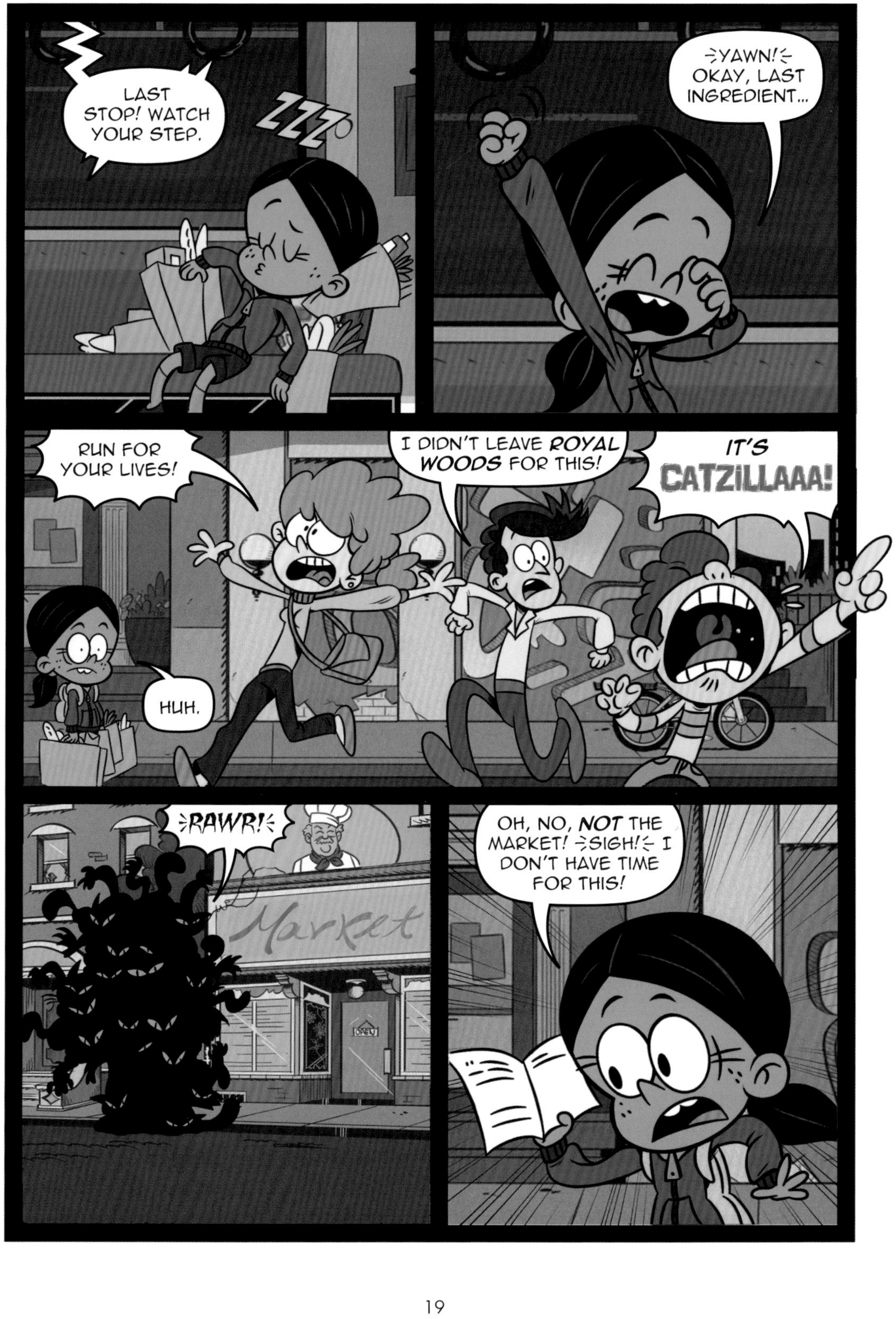
LAST STOP! WATCH YOUR STEP.
ZZZ
⇒YAWN!⇐ OKAY, LAST INGREDIENT...
RUN FOR YOUR LIVES!
I DIDN'T LEAVE ROYAL WOODS FOR THIS!
IT'S CATZILLAAA!
HUH.
⇒RAWR!⇐
Market
OPEN
OH, NO, NOT THE MARKET! ⇒SIGH!⇐ I DON'T HAVE TIME FOR THIS!

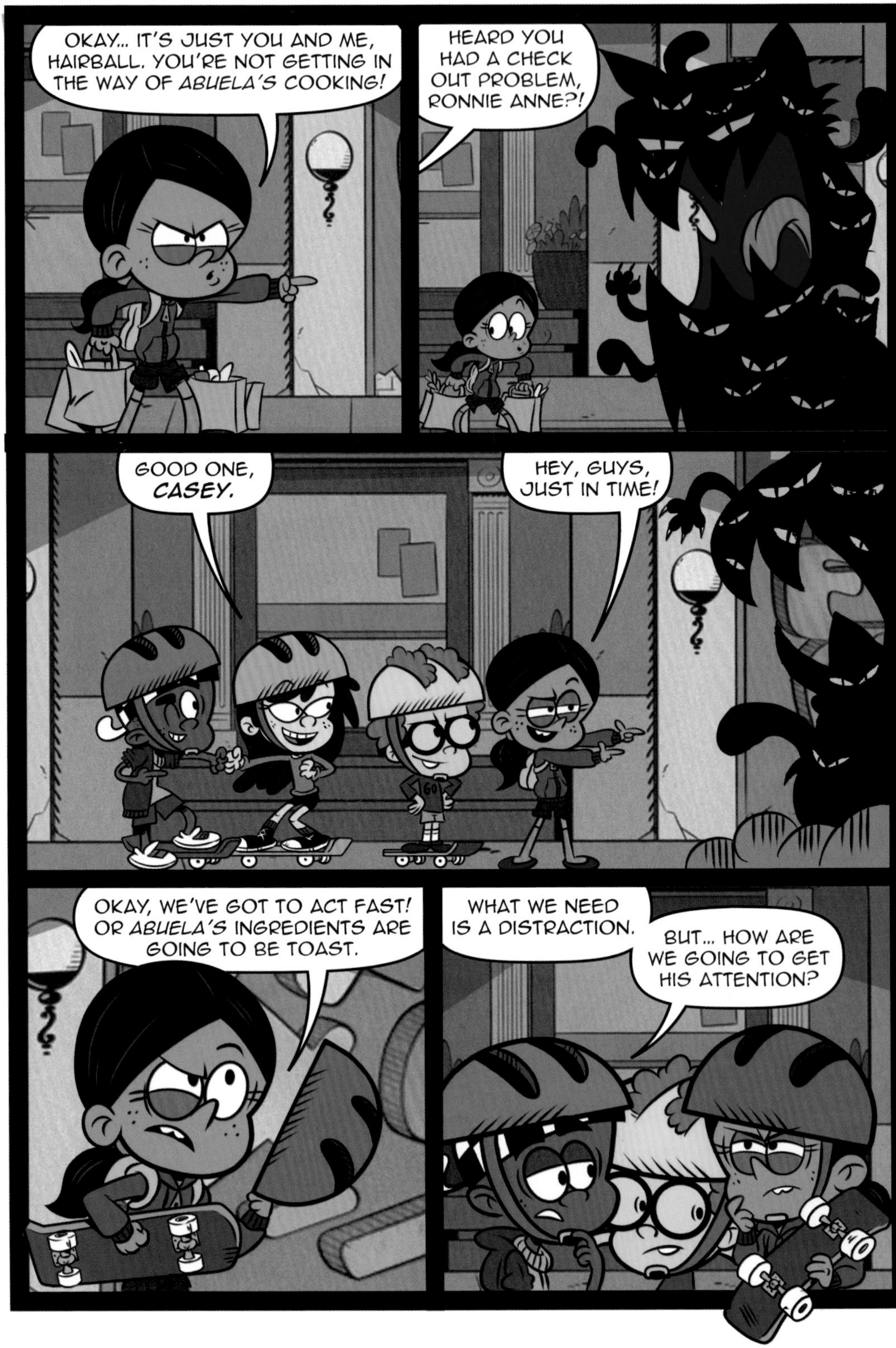
OKAY... IT'S JUST YOU AND ME, HAIRBALL. YOU'RE NOT GETTING IN THE WAY OF *ABUELA'S* COOKING!
HEARD YOU HAD A CHECK OUT PROBLEM, RONNIE ANNE?!
GOOD ONE, *CASEY.*
HEY, GUYS, JUST IN TIME!
OKAY, WE'VE GOT TO ACT FAST! OR *ABUELA'S* INGREDIENTS ARE GOING TO BE TOAST.
WHAT WE NEED IS A DISTRACTION.
BUT... HOW ARE WE GOING TO GET HIS ATTENTION?
GO

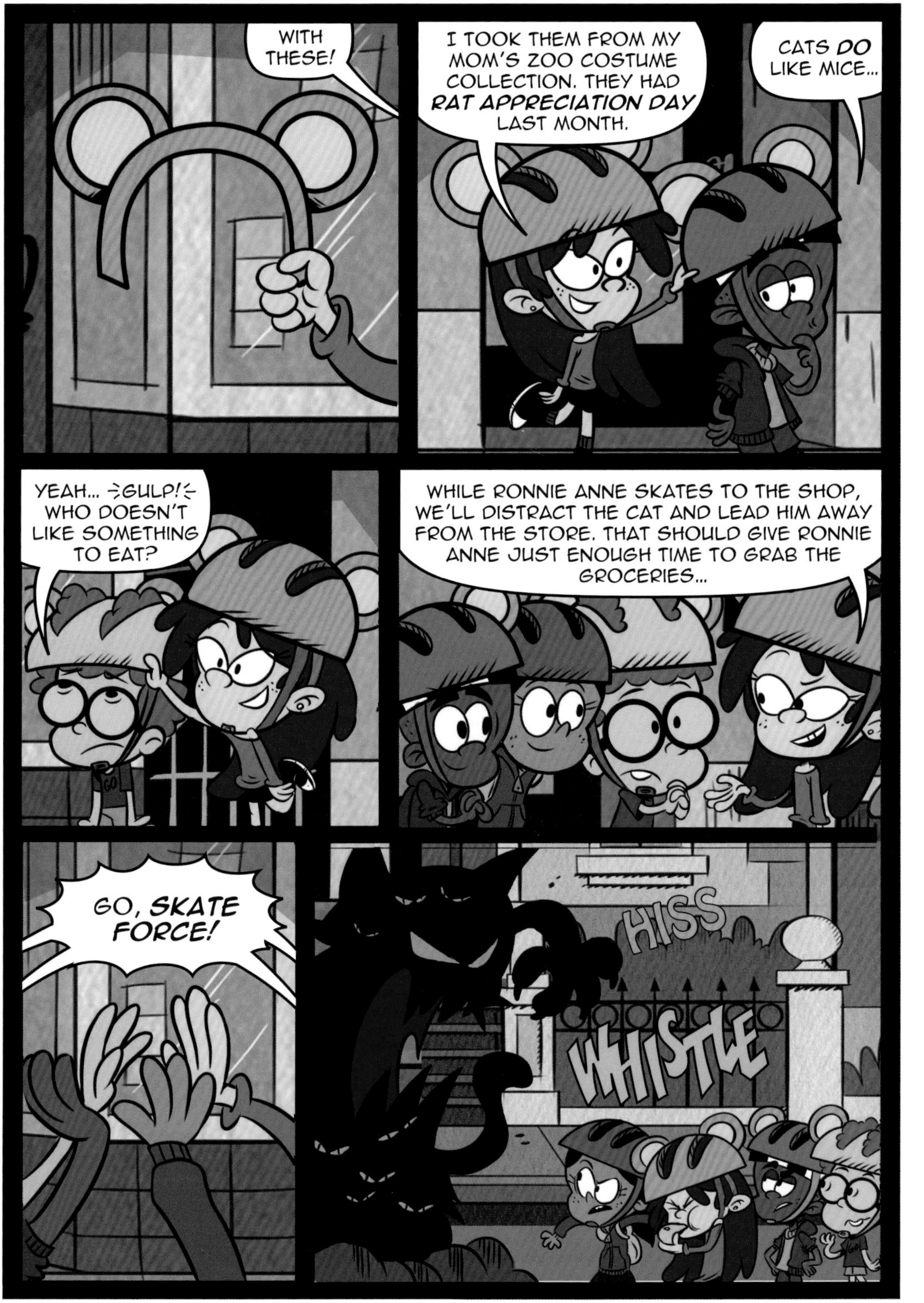
WITH THESE!
I TOOK THEM FROM MY MOM'S ZOO COSTUME COLLECTION. THEY HAD *RAT APPRECIATION DAY* LAST MONTH.
CATS *DO* LIKE MICE...
YEAH... GULP! WHO DOESN'T LIKE SOMETHING TO EAT?
WHILE RONNIE ANNE SKATES TO THE SHOP, WE'LL DISTRACT THE CAT AND LEAD HIM AWAY FROM THE STORE. THAT SHOULD GIVE RONNIE ANNE JUST ENOUGH TIME TO GRAB THE GROCERIES...
GO, *SKATE FORCE!*
HISS
WHISTLE

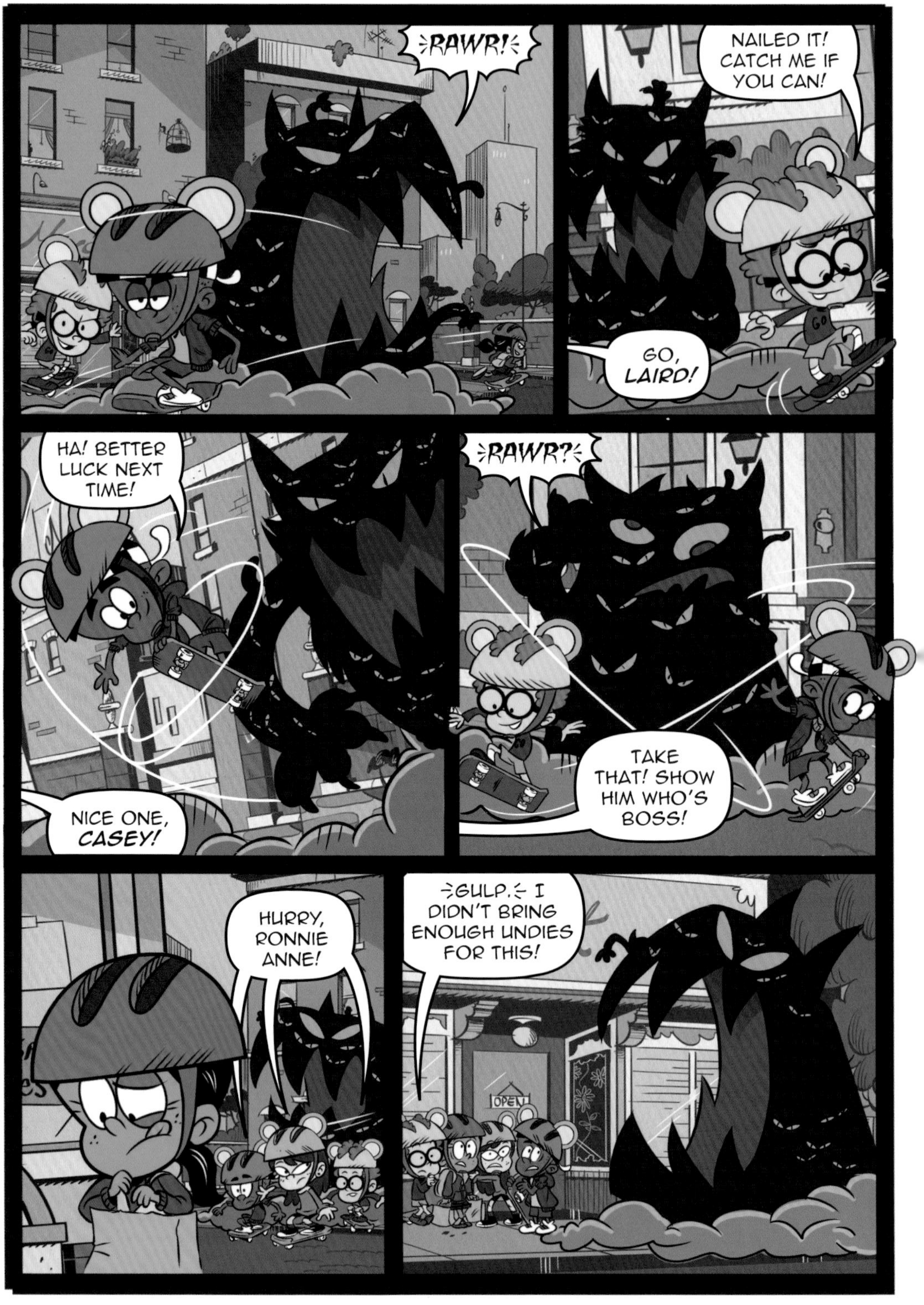
RAWR!
NAILED IT! CATCH ME IF YOU CAN!
GO, LAIRD!
HA! BETTER LUCK NEXT TIME!
NICE ONE, CASEY!
RAWR?
TAKE THAT! SHOW HIM WHO'S BOSS!
HURRY, RONNIE ANNE!
GULP. I DIDN'T BRING ENOUGH UNDIES FOR THIS!
OPEN

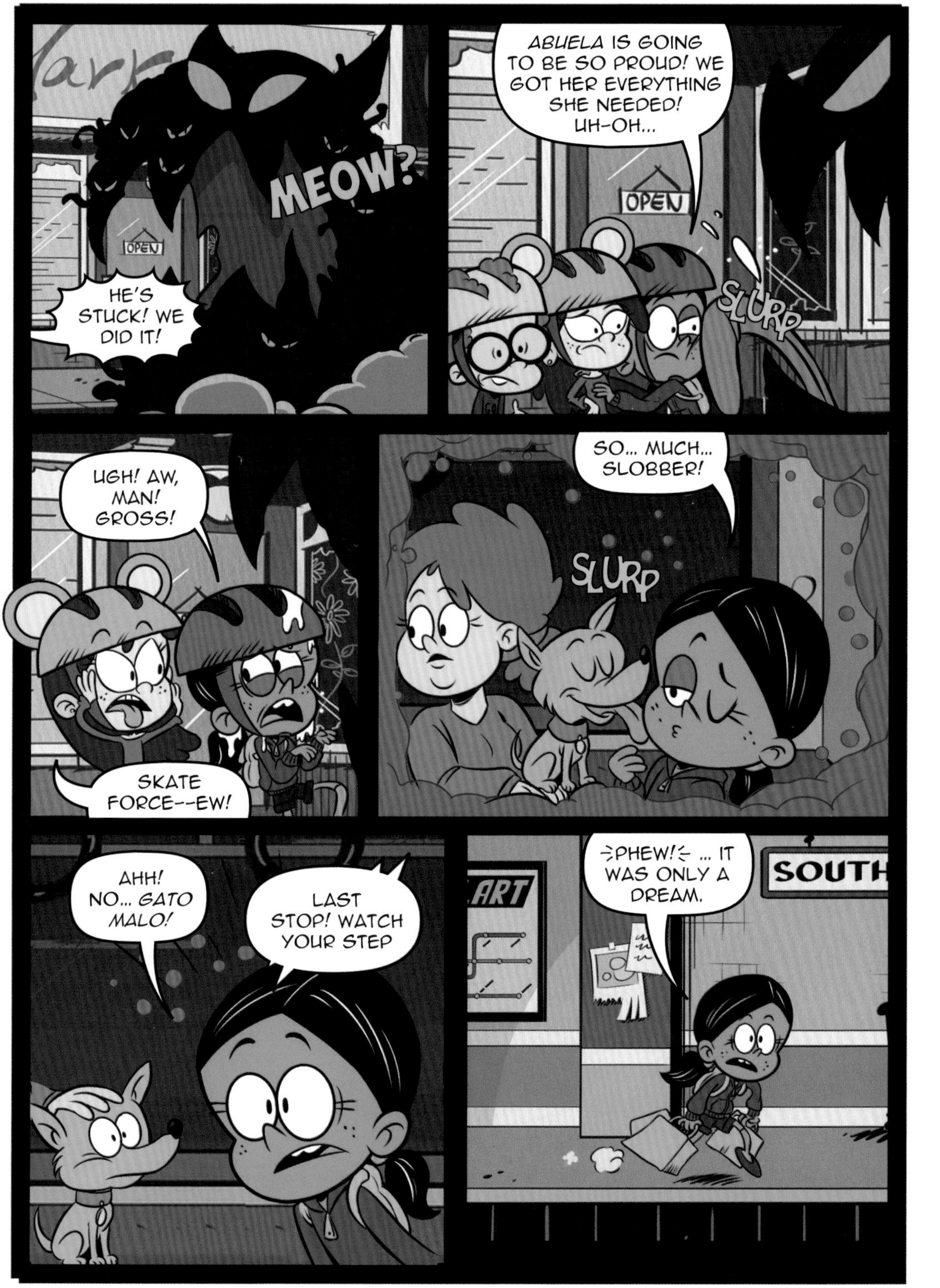
MEOW?
HE'S STUCK! WE DID IT!
ABUELA IS GOING TO BE SO PROUD! WE GOT HER EVERYTHING SHE NEEDED! UH-OH...
OPEN
SLURP
UGH! AW, MAN! GROSS!
SKATE FORCE--EW!
SO... MUCH... SLOBBER!
SLURP
AHH! NO... GATO MALO!
LAST STOP! WATCH YOUR STEP
PHEW! ... IT WAS ONLY A DREAM.
SOUTH

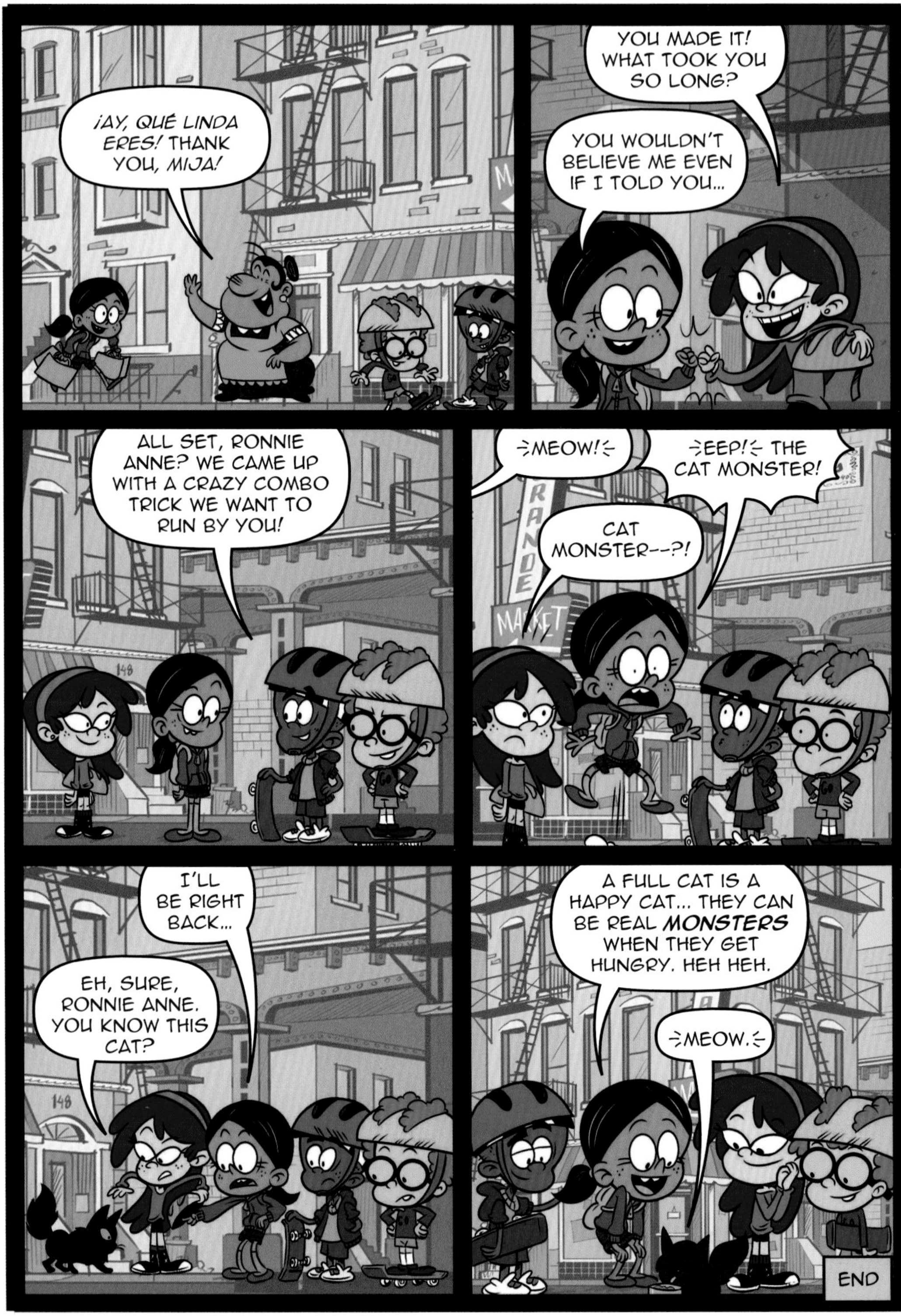
¡AY, QUÉ LINDA ERES! THANK YOU, MIJA!
YOU MADE IT! WHAT TOOK YOU SO LONG?
YOU WOULDN'T BELIEVE ME EVEN IF I TOLD YOU...
ALL SET, RONNIE ANNE? WE CAME UP WITH A CRAZY COMBO TRICK WE WANT TO RUN BY YOU!
MEOW!
EEP! THE CAT MONSTER!
CAT MONSTER--?!
I'LL BE RIGHT BACK...
EH, SURE, RONNIE ANNE. YOU KNOW THIS CAT?
A FULL CAT IS A HAPPY CAT... THEY CAN BE REAL MONSTERS WHEN THEY GET HUNGRY. HEH HEH.
MEOW.
END

"TOUGH HOOKY"

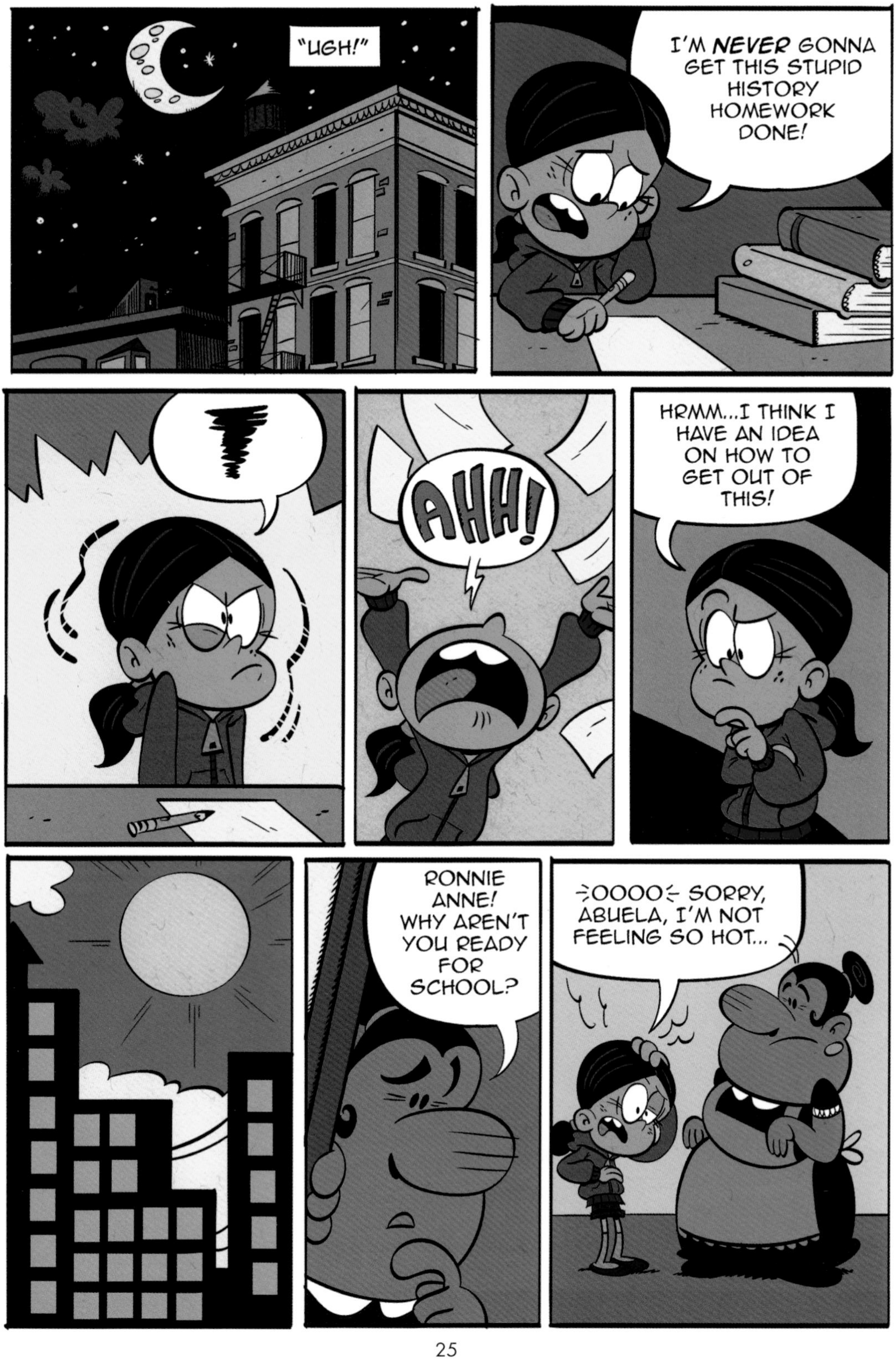
"UGH!"
I'M *NEVER* GONNA GET THIS STUPID HISTORY HOMEWORK DONE!
AHH!
HRMM...I THINK I HAVE AN IDEA ON HOW TO GET OUT OF THIS!
RONNIE ANNE! WHY AREN'T YOU READY FOR SCHOOL?
OOOO SORRY, ABUELA, I'M NOT FEELING SO HOT...

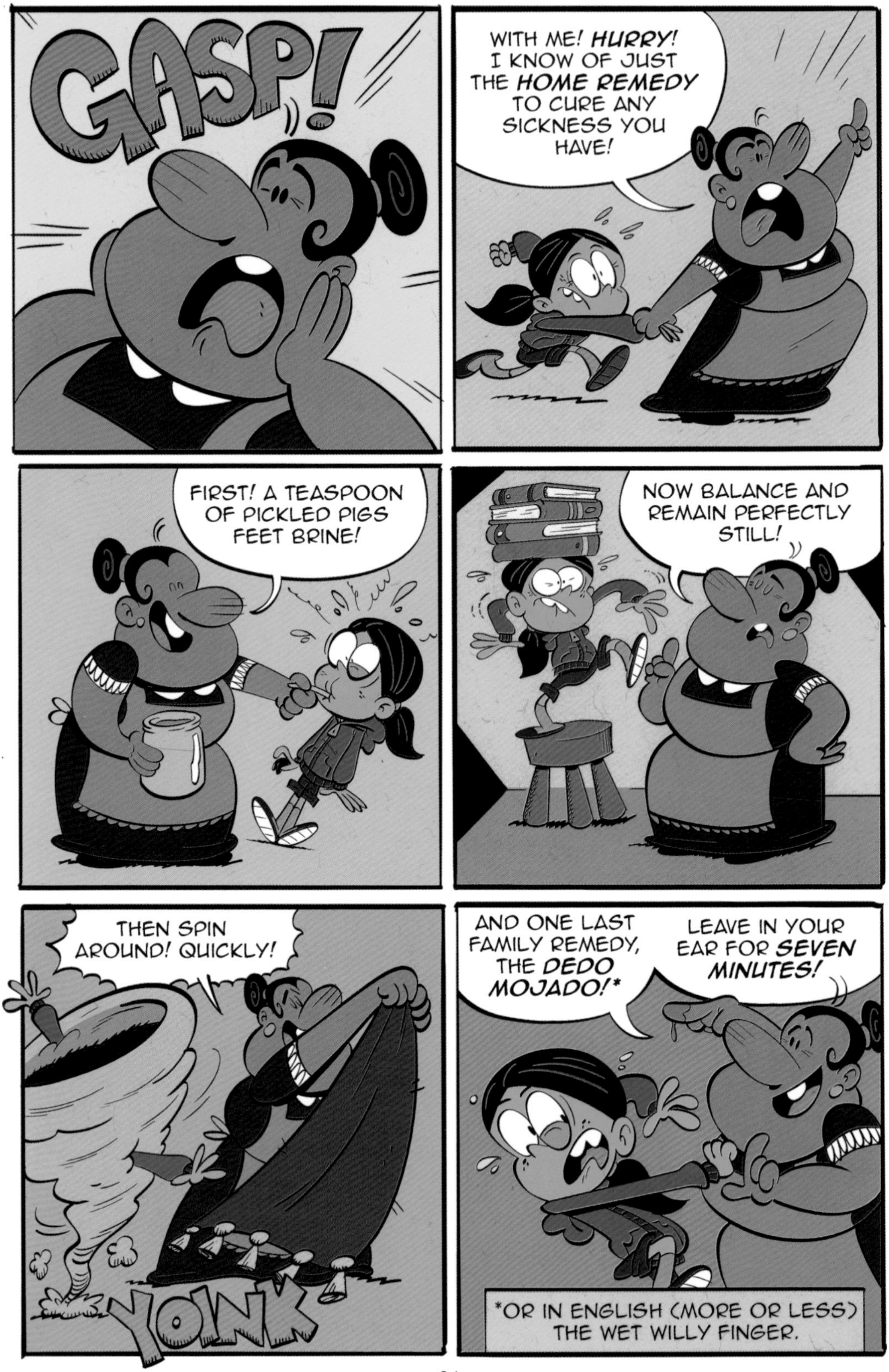
GASP!
WITH ME! HURRY! I KNOW OF JUST THE HOME REMEDY TO CURE ANY SICKNESS YOU HAVE!
FIRST! A TEASPOON OF PICKLED PIGS FEET BRINE!
NOW BALANCE AND REMAIN PERFECTLY STILL!
THEN SPIN AROUND! QUICKLY!
YOINK
AND ONE LAST FAMILY REMEDY, THE DEDO MOJADO!*
LEAVE IN YOUR EAR FOR SEVEN MINUTES!
*OR IN ENGLISH (MORE OR LESS) THE WET WILLY FINGER.

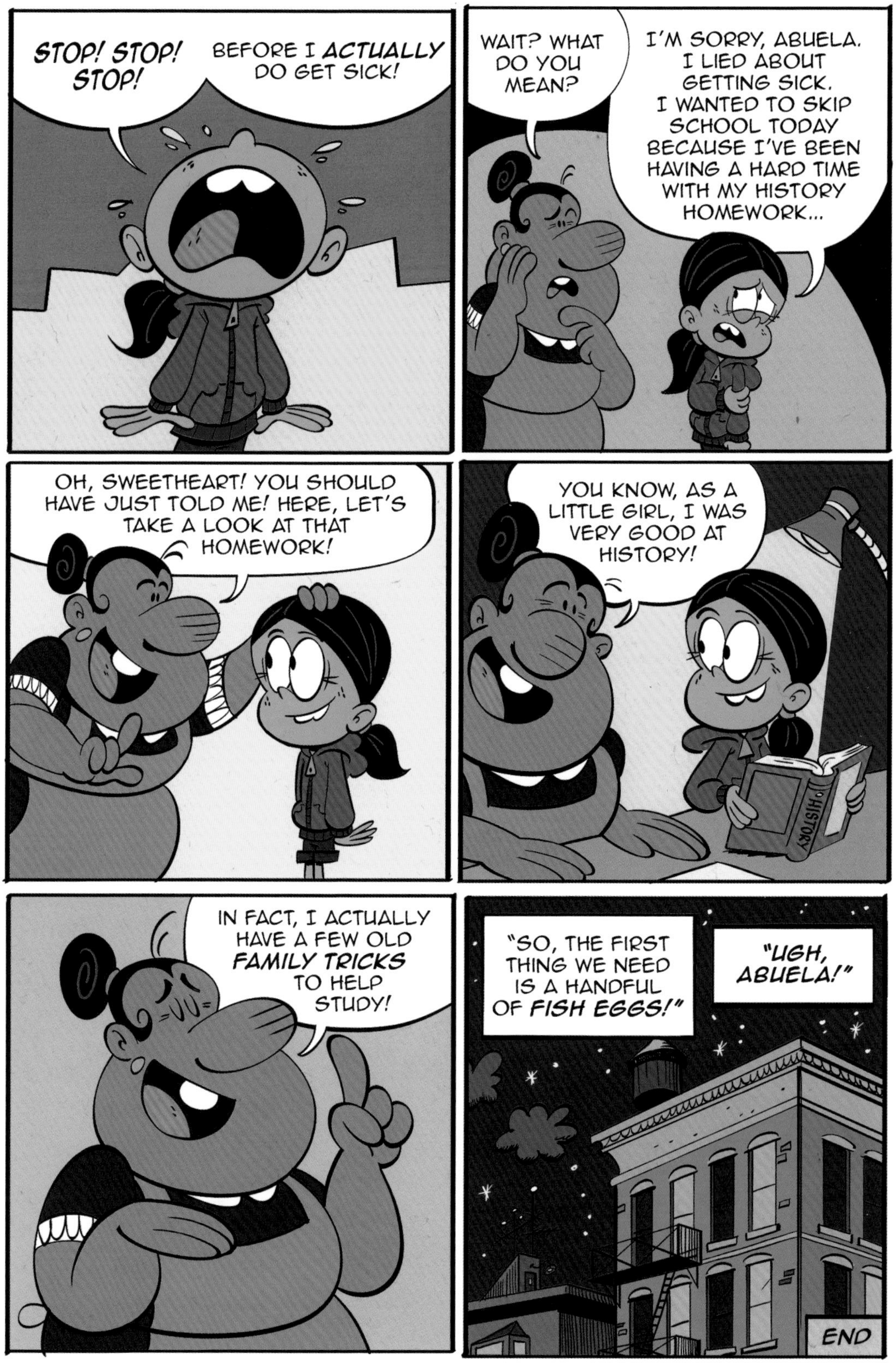
STOP! STOP! STOP!
BEFORE I ACTUALLY DO GET SICK!
WAIT? WHAT DO YOU MEAN?
I'M SORRY, ABUELA. I LIED ABOUT GETTING SICK. I WANTED TO SKIP SCHOOL TODAY BECAUSE I'VE BEEN HAVING A HARD TIME WITH MY HISTORY HOMEWORK...
OH, SWEETHEART! YOU SHOULD HAVE JUST TOLD ME! HERE, LET'S TAKE A LOOK AT THAT HOMEWORK!
YOU KNOW, AS A LITTLE GIRL, I WAS VERY GOOD AT HISTORY!
HISTORY
IN FACT, I ACTUALLY HAVE A FEW OLD FAMILY TRICKS TO HELP STUDY!
"SO, THE FIRST THING WE NEED IS A HANDFUL OF FISH EGGS!"
"UGH, ABUELA!"
END

"THE GREAT ESCAPE"

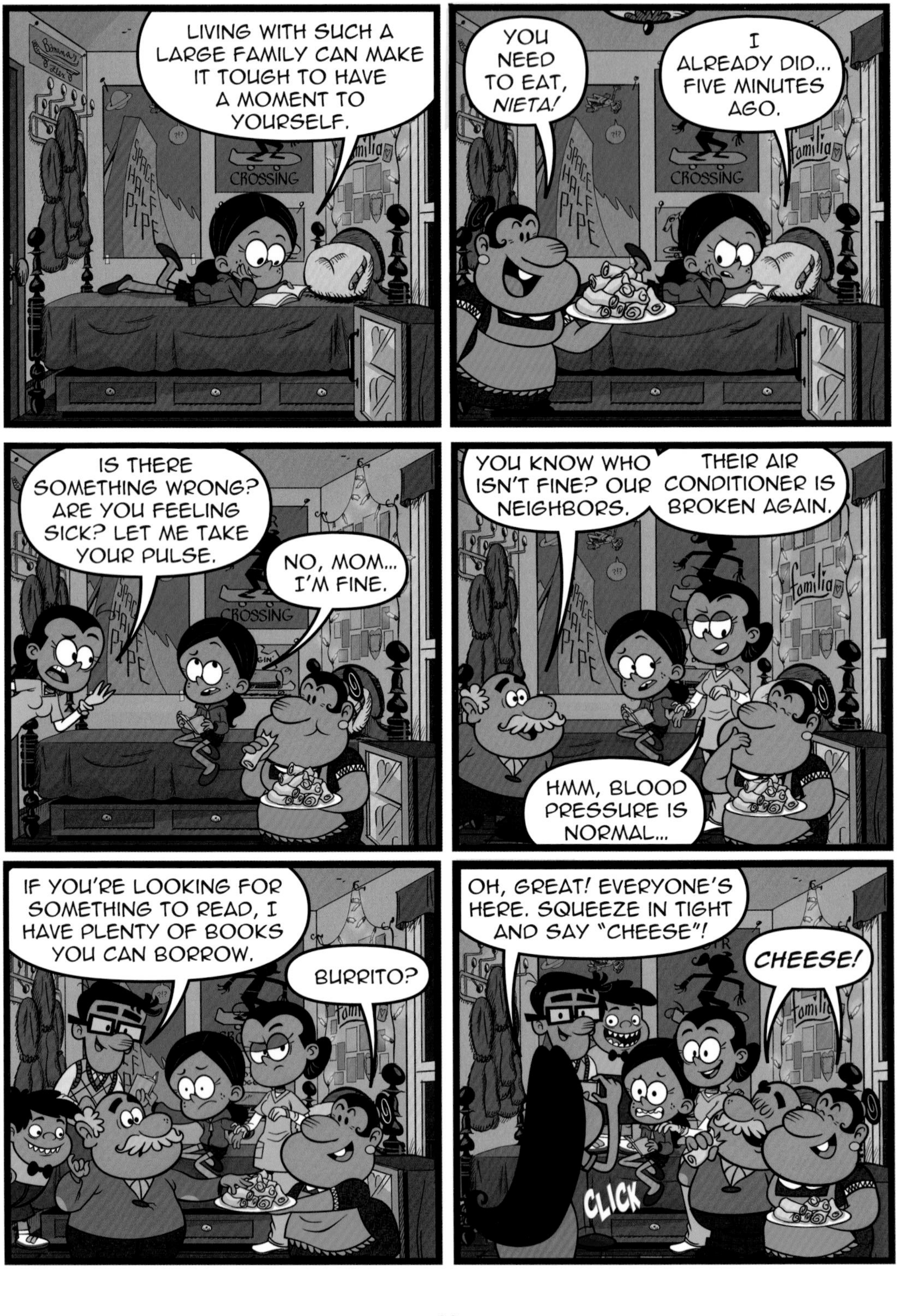
LIVING WITH SUCH A LARGE FAMILY CAN MAKE IT TOUGH TO HAVE A MOMENT TO YOURSELF.
YOU NEED TO EAT, NIETA!
I ALREADY DID... FIVE MINUTES AGO.
IS THERE SOMETHING WRONG? ARE YOU FEELING SICK? LET ME TAKE YOUR PULSE.
NO, MOM... I'M FINE.
YOU KNOW WHO ISN'T FINE? OUR NEIGHBORS.
THEIR AIR CONDITIONER IS BROKEN AGAIN.
HMM, BLOOD PRESSURE IS NORMAL...
IF YOU'RE LOOKING FOR SOMETHING TO READ, I HAVE PLENTY OF BOOKS YOU CAN BORROW.
BURRITO?
OH, GREAT! EVERYONE'S HERE. SQUEEZE IN TIGHT AND SAY "CHEESE"!
CHEESE!
CLICK

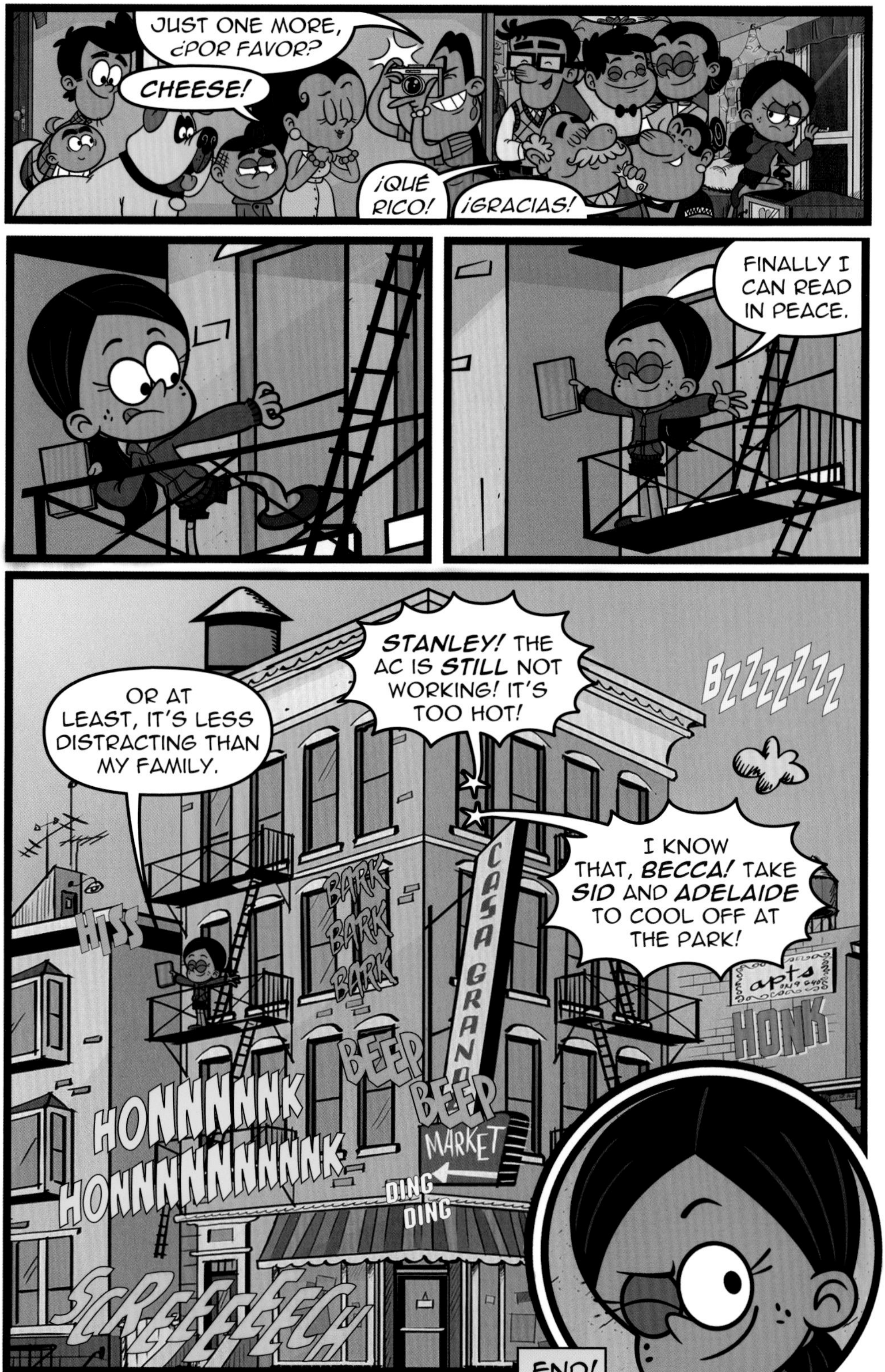
JUST ONE MORE, ¿POR FAVOR?
CHEESE!
¡QUÉ RICO!
¡GRACIAS!
FINALLY I CAN READ IN PEACE.
OR AT LEAST, IT'S LESS DISTRACTING THAN MY FAMILY.
STANLEY! THE AC IS STILL NOT WORKING! IT'S TOO HOT!
BZZZZZZZ
I KNOW THAT, BECCA! TAKE SID AND ADELAIDE TO COOL OFF AT THE PARK!
HISS
BARK BARK BARK
CASA GRAND
apts
HONK
BEEP BEEP
HONNNNNK HONNNNNNNNNK
MARKET
DING DING
SCREEEEECH
END!

"MAYBE IT'S NATURAL"

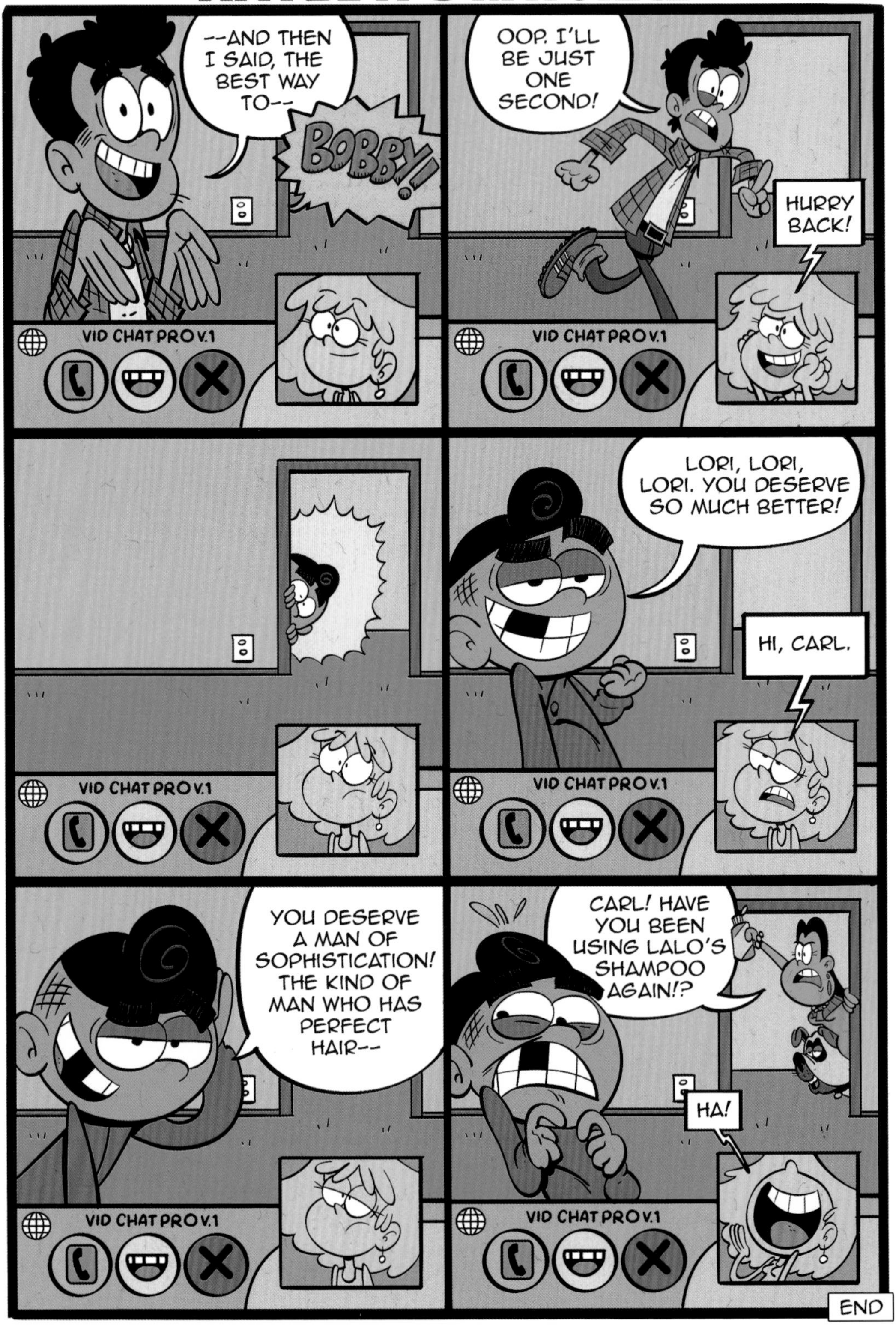
--AND THEN I SAID, THE BEST WAY TO--
BOBBY!
VID CHAT PRO V.1
OOP. I'LL BE JUST ONE SECOND!
HURRY BACK!
VID CHAT PRO V.1
VID CHAT PRO V.1
LORI, LORI, LORI. YOU DESERVE SO MUCH BETTER!
HI, CARL.
VID CHAT PRO V.1
YOU DESERVE A MAN OF SOPHISTICATION! THE KIND OF MAN WHO HAS PERFECT HAIR--
VID CHAT PRO V.1
CARL! HAVE YOU BEEN USING LALO'S SHAMPOO AGAIN!?
HA!
VID CHAT PRO V.1
END

"WORKED UP"

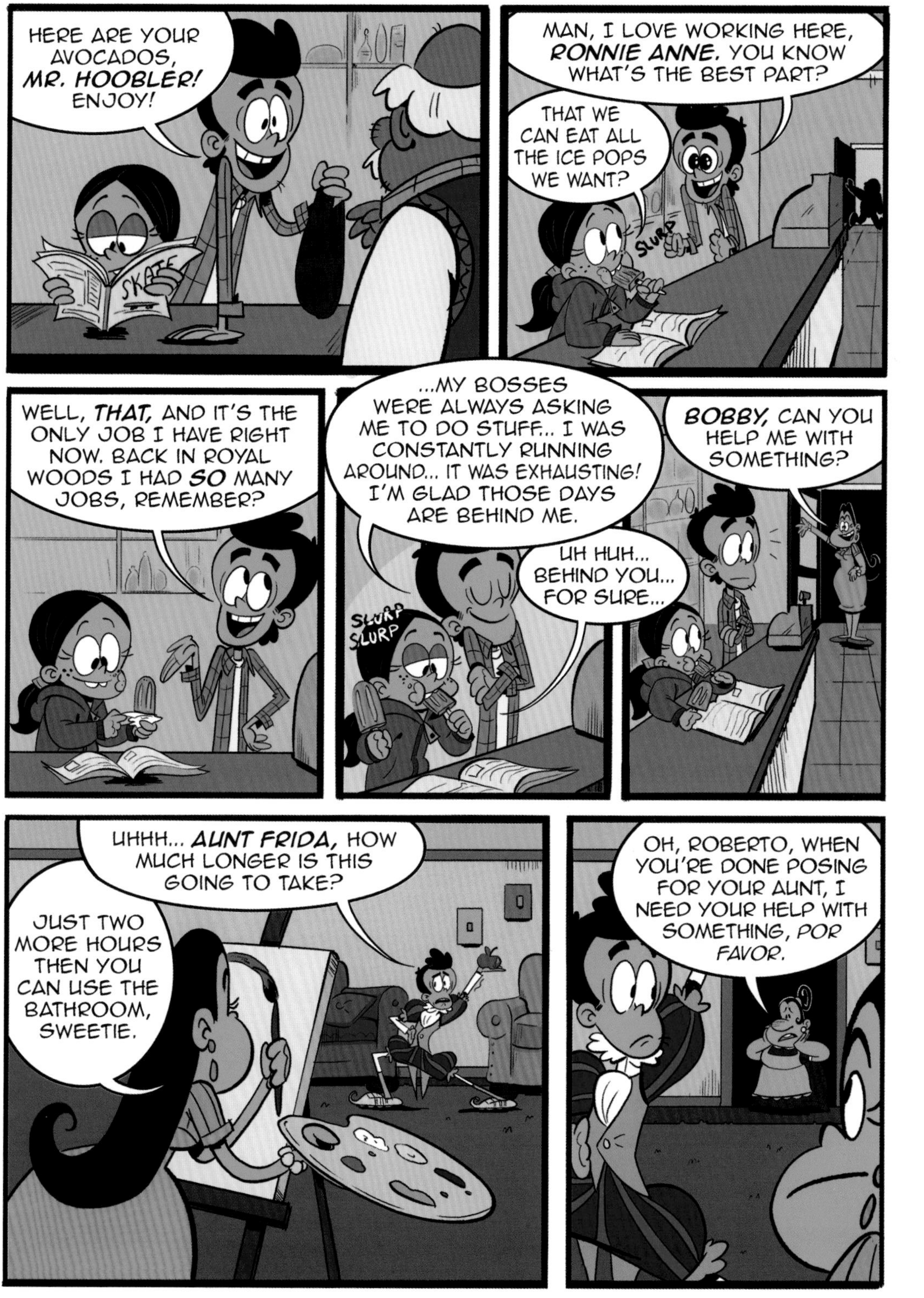
HERE ARE YOUR AVOCADOS, MR. HOOBLER! ENJOY!
SKATE
MAN, I LOVE WORKING HERE, RONNIE ANNE. YOU KNOW WHAT'S THE BEST PART?
THAT WE CAN EAT ALL THE ICE POPS WE WANT?
SLURP
WELL, THAT, AND IT'S THE ONLY JOB I HAVE RIGHT NOW. BACK IN ROYAL WOODS I HAD SO MANY JOBS, REMEMBER?
...MY BOSSES WERE ALWAYS ASKING ME TO DO STUFF... I WAS CONSTANTLY RUNNING AROUND... IT WAS EXHAUSTING! I'M GLAD THOSE DAYS ARE BEHIND ME.
UH HUH... BEHIND YOU... FOR SURE...
SLURP SLURP
BOBBY, CAN YOU HELP ME WITH SOMETHING?
UHHH... AUNT FRIDA, HOW MUCH LONGER IS THIS GOING TO TAKE?
JUST TWO MORE HOURS THEN YOU CAN USE THE BATHROOM, SWEETIE.
OH, ROBERTO, WHEN YOU'RE DONE POSING FOR YOUR AUNT, I NEED YOUR HELP WITH SOMETHING, POR FAVOR.

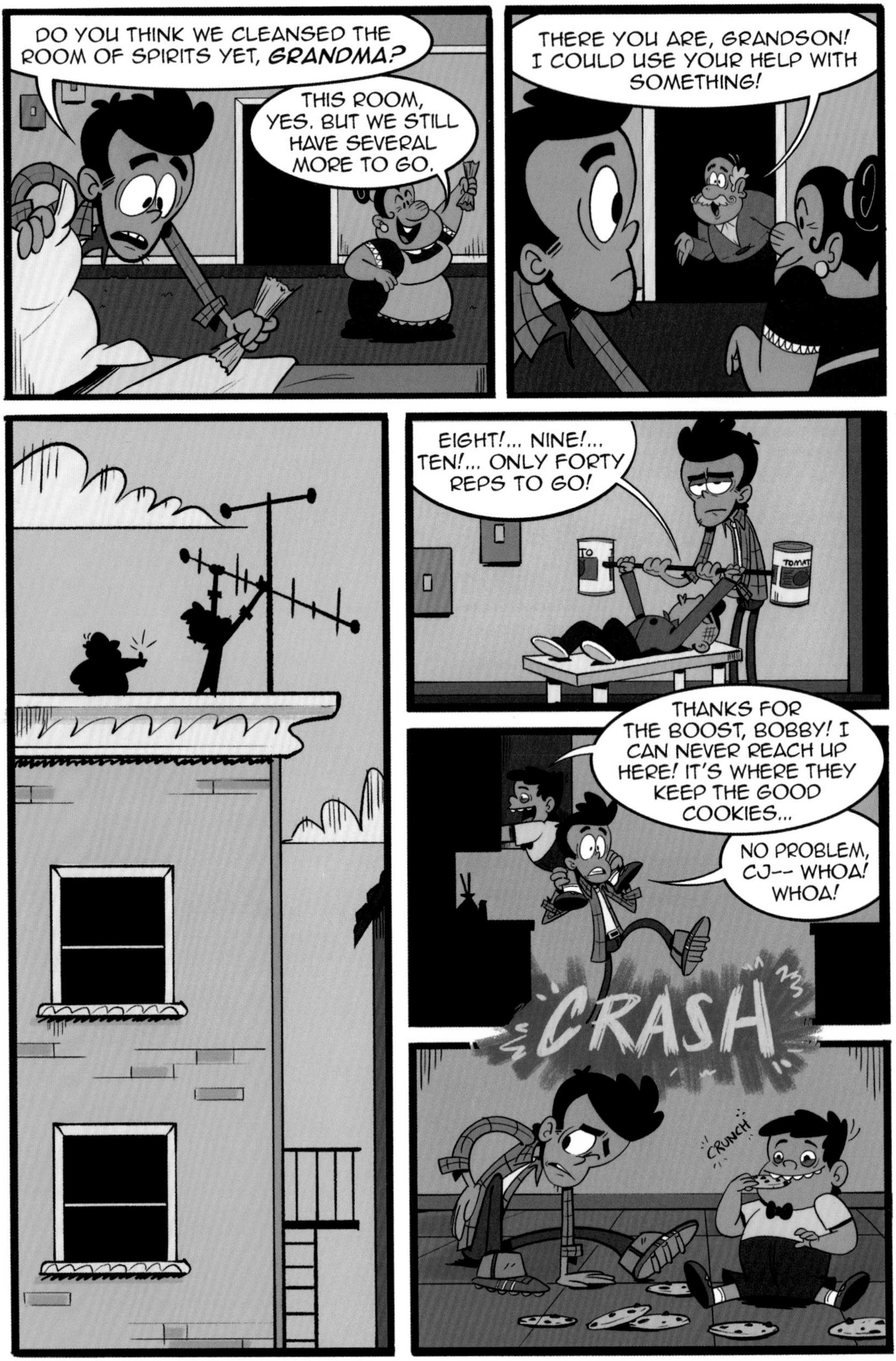
DO YOU THINK WE CLEANSED THE ROOM OF SPIRITS YET, GRANDMA?
THIS ROOM, YES. BUT WE STILL HAVE SEVERAL MORE TO GO.
THERE YOU ARE, GRANDSON! I COULD USE YOUR HELP WITH SOMETHING!
EIGHT!... NINE!... TEN!... ONLY FORTY REPS TO GO!
THANKS FOR THE BOOST, BOBBY! I CAN NEVER REACH UP HERE! IT'S WHERE THEY KEEP THE GOOD COOKIES...
NO PROBLEM, CJ-- WHOA! WHOA!
CRASH
CRUNCH

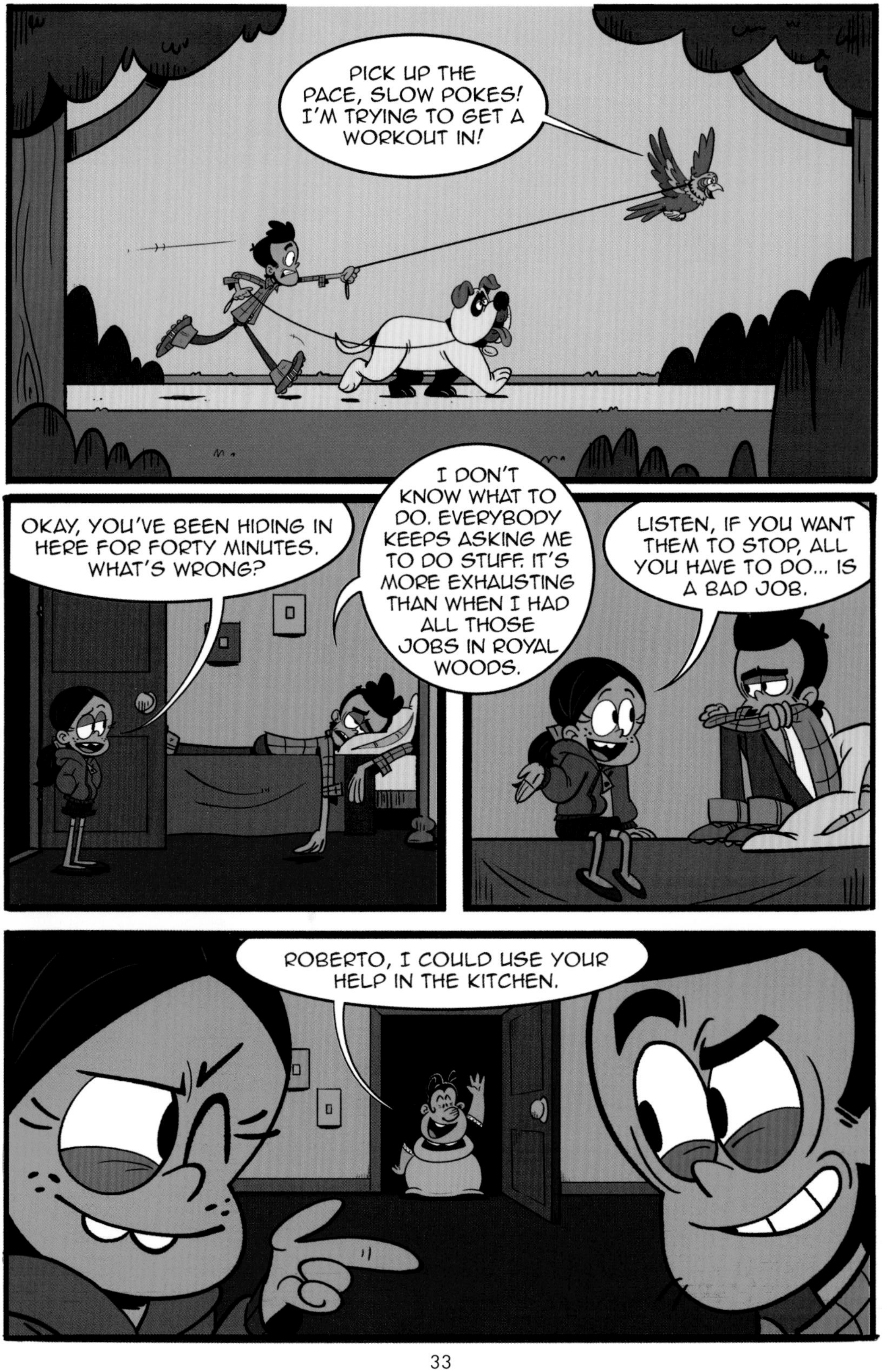
PICK UP THE PACE, SLOW POKES! I'M TRYING TO GET A WORKOUT IN!
OKAY, YOU'VE BEEN HIDING IN HERE FOR FORTY MINUTES. WHAT'S WRONG?
I DON'T KNOW WHAT TO DO. EVERYBODY KEEPS ASKING ME TO DO STUFF. IT'S MORE EXHAUSTING THAN WHEN I HAD ALL THOSE JOBS IN ROYAL WOODS.
LISTEN, IF YOU WANT THEM TO STOP, ALL YOU HAVE TO DO... IS A BAD JOB.
ROBERTO, I COULD USE YOUR HELP IN THE KITCHEN.

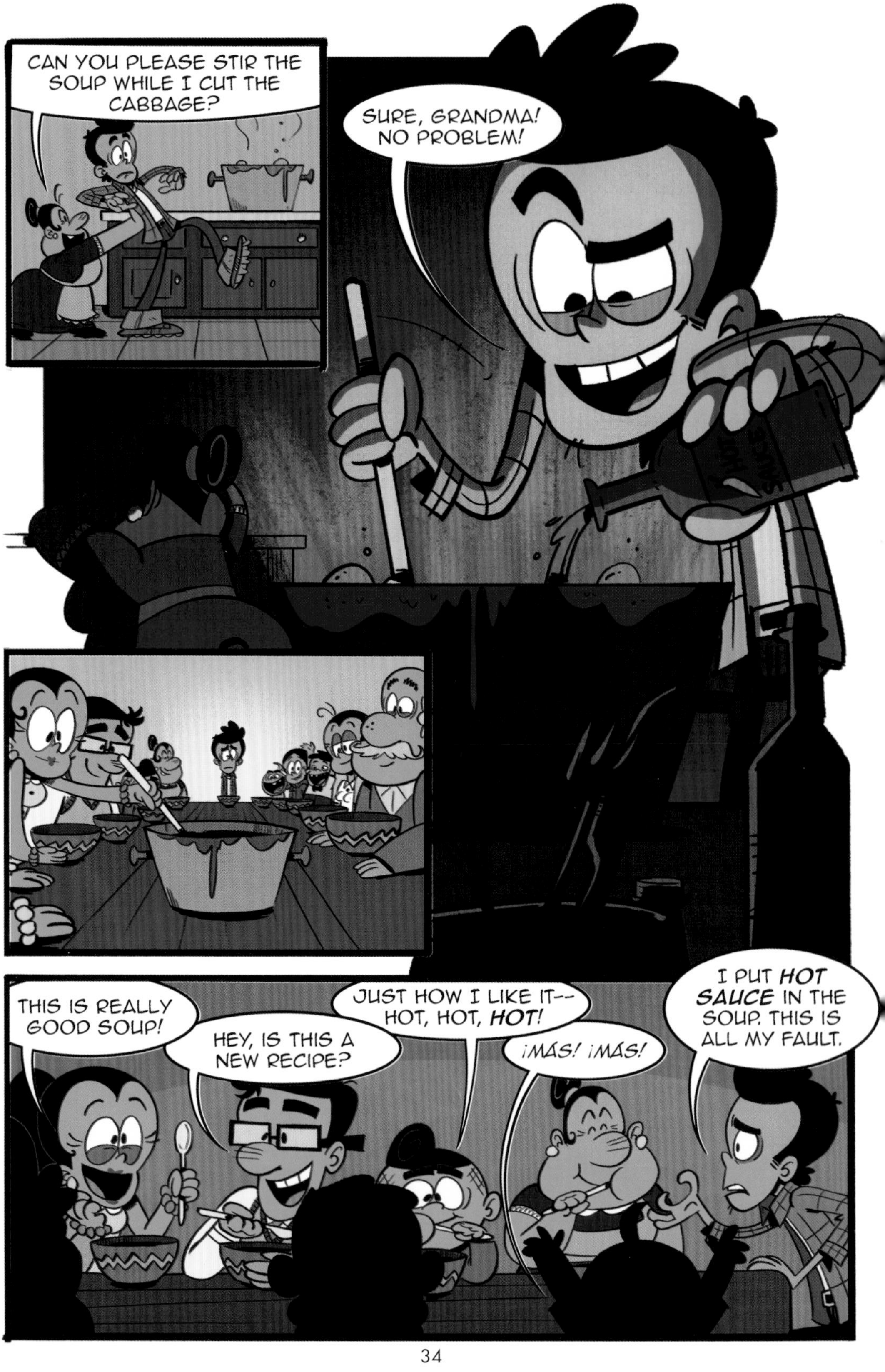

CAN YOU PLEASE STIR THE SOUP WHILE I CUT THE CABBAGE?
SURE, GRANDMA! NO PROBLEM!
THIS IS REALLY GOOD SOUP!
HEY, IS THIS A NEW RECIPE?
JUST HOW I LIKE IT-- HOT, HOT, HOT!
¡MÁS! ¡MÁS!
I PUT HOT SAUCE IN THE SOUP. THIS IS ALL MY FAULT.

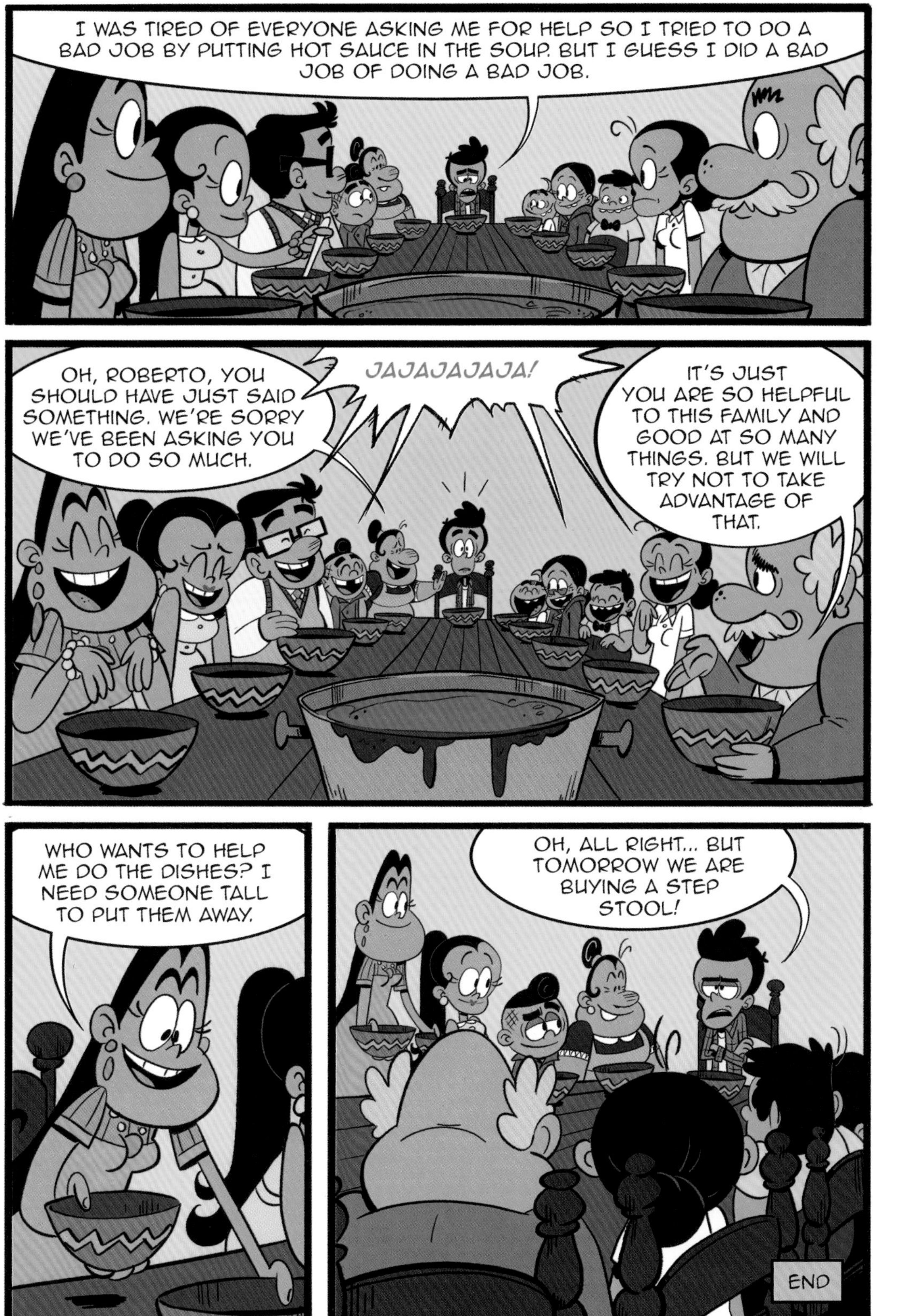

I WAS TIRED OF EVERYONE ASKING ME FOR HELP SO I TRIED TO DO A BAD JOB BY PUTTING HOT SAUCE IN THE SOUP. BUT I GUESS I DID A BAD JOB OF DOING A BAD JOB.
OH, ROBERTO, YOU SHOULD HAVE JUST SAID SOMETHING. WE'RE SORRY WE'VE BEEN ASKING YOU TO DO SO MUCH.
JAJAJAJAJA!
IT'S JUST YOU ARE SO HELPFUL TO THIS FAMILY AND GOOD AT SO MANY THINGS. BUT WE WILL TRY NOT TO TAKE ADVANTAGE OF THAT.
WHO WANTS TO HELP ME DO THE DISHES? I NEED SOMEONE TALL TO PUT THEM AWAY.
OH, ALL RIGHT... BUT TOMORROW WE ARE BUYING A STEP STOOL!
END

"BABES IN THE CITY"

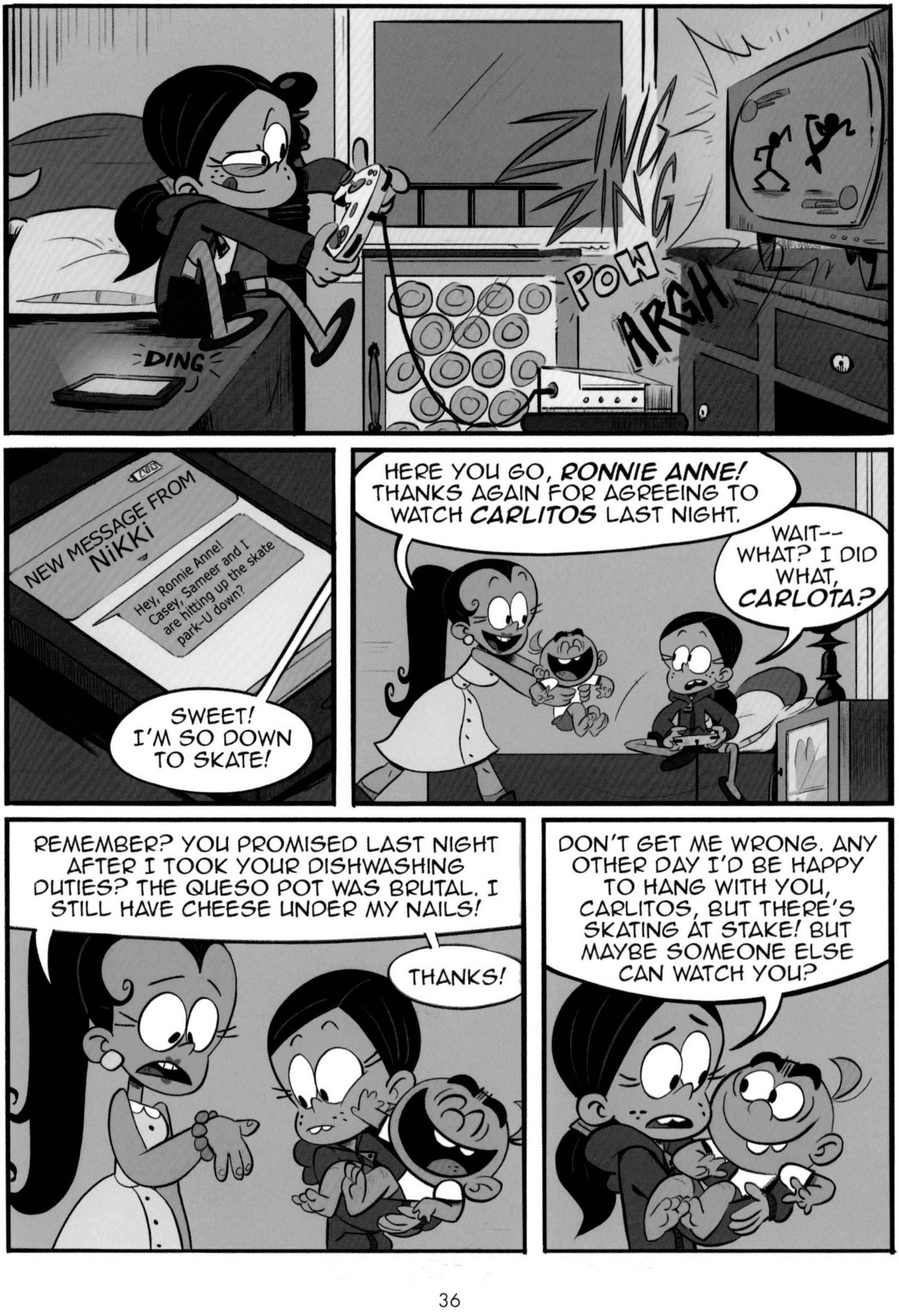
ZING
ZING
POW
ARGH
DING
NEW MESSAGE FROM
NiKKi
Hey, Ronnie Anne! Casey, Sameer and I are hitting up the skate park–U down?
SWEET! I'M SO DOWN TO SKATE!
HERE YOU GO, RONNIE ANNE! THANKS AGAIN FOR AGREEING TO WATCH CARLITOS LAST NIGHT.
WAIT-- WHAT? I DID WHAT, CARLOTA?
REMEMBER? YOU PROMISED LAST NIGHT AFTER I TOOK YOUR DISHWASHING DUTIES? THE QUESO POT WAS BRUTAL. I STILL HAVE CHEESE UNDER MY NAILS!
THANKS!
DON'T GET ME WRONG. ANY OTHER DAY I'D BE HAPPY TO HANG WITH YOU, CARLITOS, BUT THERE'S SKATING AT STAKE! BUT MAYBE SOMEONE ELSE CAN WATCH YOU?

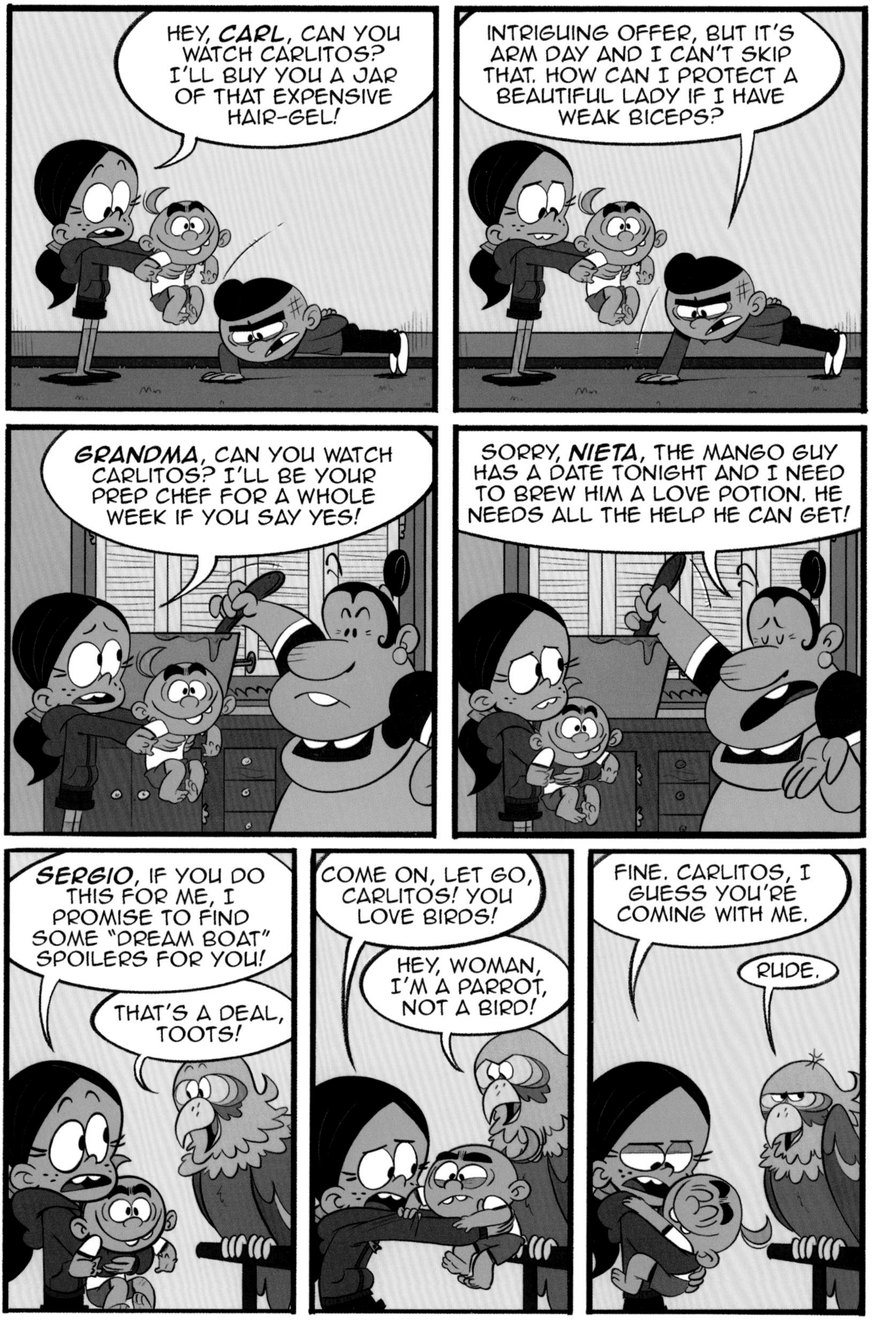
HEY, CARL, CAN YOU WATCH CARLITOS? I'LL BUY YOU A JAR OF THAT EXPENSIVE HAIR-GEL!
INTRIGUING OFFER, BUT IT'S ARM DAY AND I CAN'T SKIP THAT. HOW CAN I PROTECT A BEAUTIFUL LADY IF I HAVE WEAK BICEPS?
GRANDMA, CAN YOU WATCH CARLITOS? I'LL BE YOUR PREP CHEF FOR A WHOLE WEEK IF YOU SAY YES!
SORRY, NIETA, THE MANGO GUY HAS A DATE TONIGHT AND I NEED TO BREW HIM A LOVE POTION. HE NEEDS ALL THE HELP HE CAN GET!
SERGIO, IF YOU DO THIS FOR ME, I PROMISE TO FIND SOME "DREAM BOAT" SPOILERS FOR YOU!
THAT'S A DEAL, TOOTS!
COME ON, LET GO, CARLITOS! YOU LOVE BIRDS!
HEY, WOMAN, I'M A PARROT, NOT A BIRD!
FINE. CARLITOS, I GUESS YOU'RE COMING WITH ME.
RUDE.

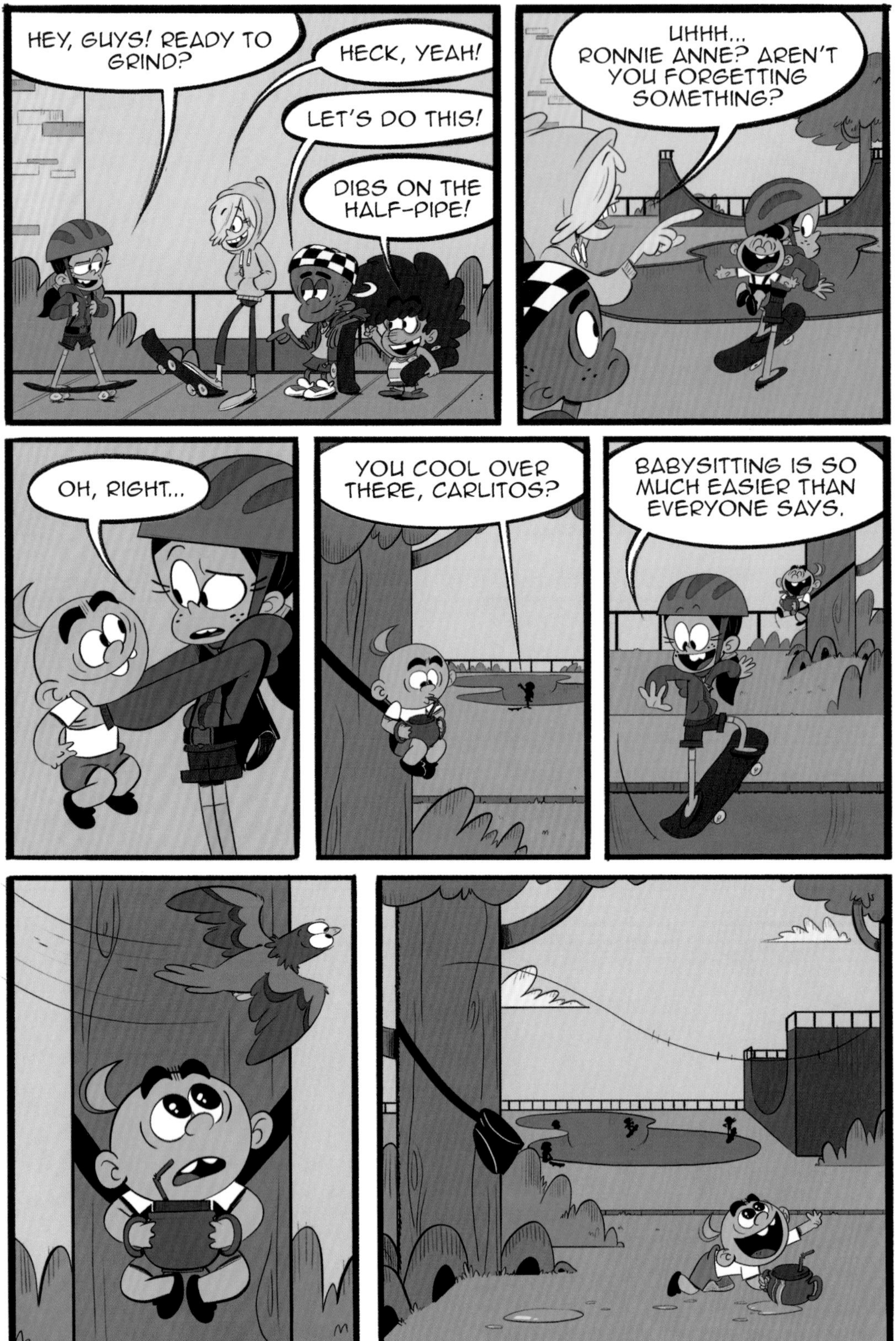
HEY, GUYS! READY TO GRIND?
HECK, YEAH!
LET'S DO THIS!
DIBS ON THE HALF-PIPE!
UHHH... RONNIE ANNE? AREN'T YOU FORGETTING SOMETHING?
OH, RIGHT...
YOU COOL OVER THERE, CARLITOS?
BABYSITTING IS SO MUCH EASIER THAN EVERYONE SAYS.

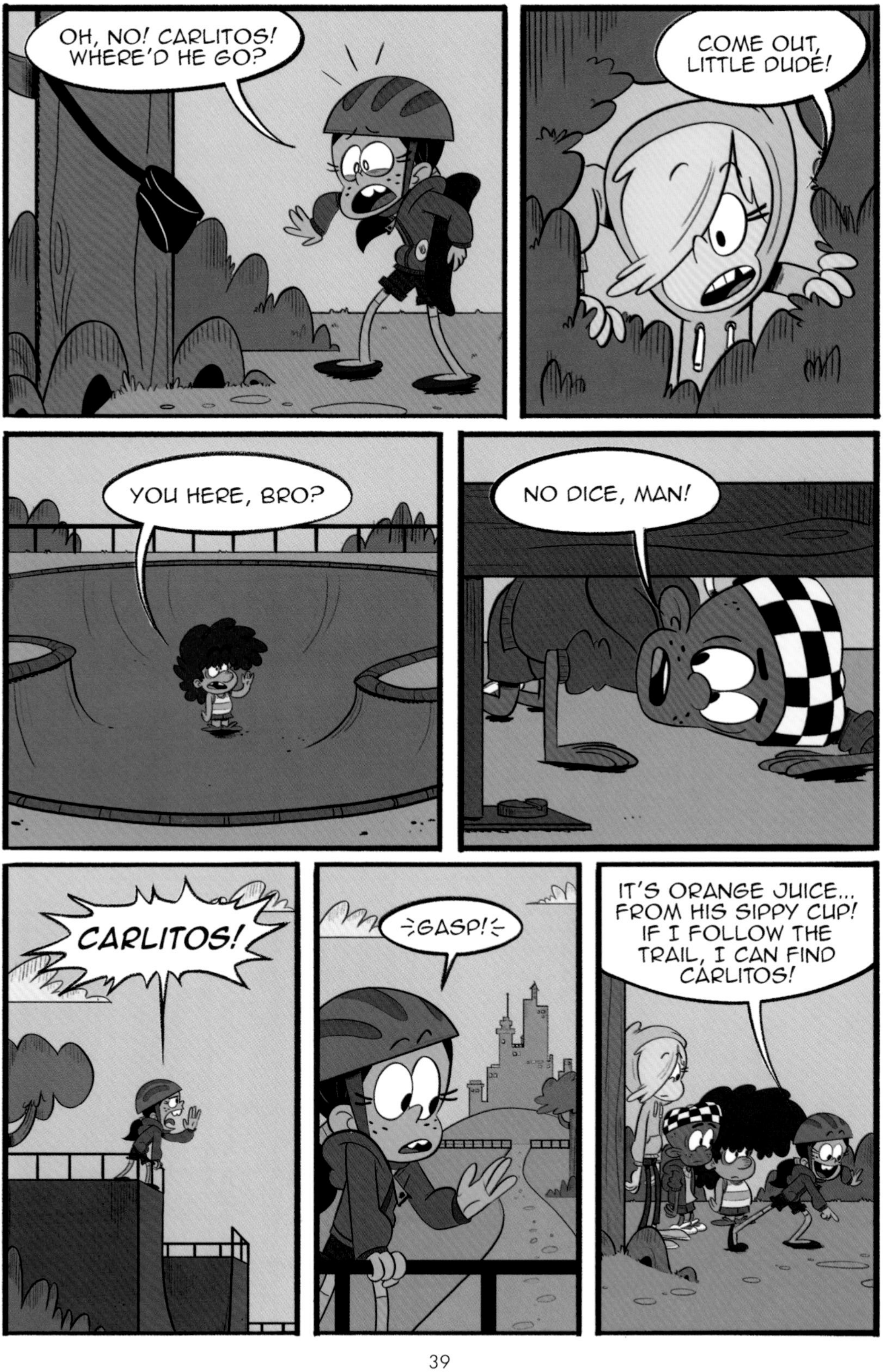
OH, NO! CARLITOS! WHERE'D HE GO?
COME OUT, LITTLE DUDE!
YOU HERE, BRO?
NO DICE, MAN!
CARLITOS!
GASP!
IT'S ORANGE JUICE... FROM HIS SIPPY CUP! IF I FOLLOW THE TRAIL, I CAN FIND CARLITOS!

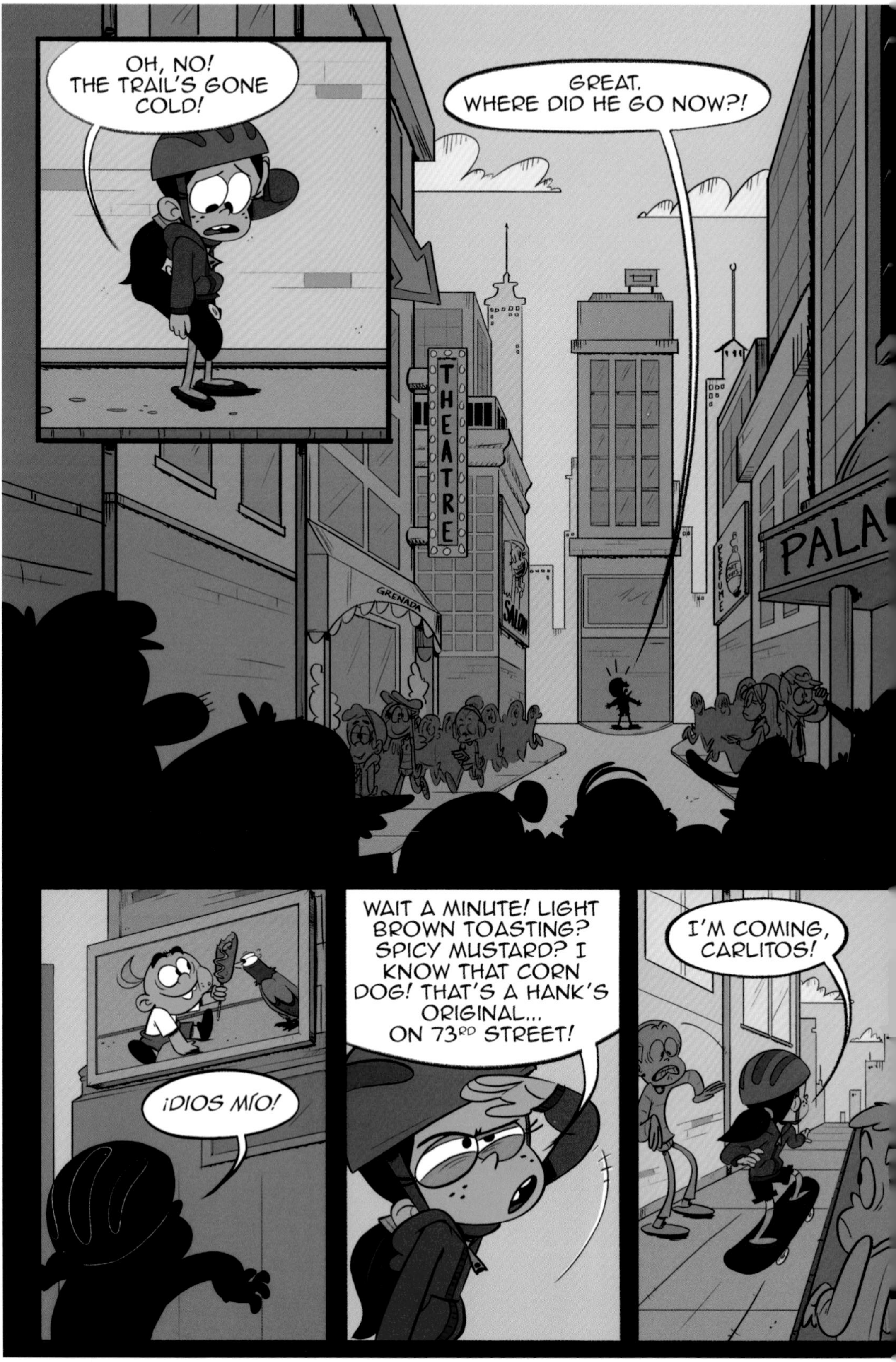
OH, NO! THE TRAIL'S GONE COLD!
GREAT. WHERE DID HE GO NOW?!
THEATRE
PALA
GRENADA
¡DIOS MÍO!
WAIT A MINUTE! LIGHT BROWN TOASTING? SPICY MUSTARD? I KNOW THAT CORN DOG! THAT'S A HANK'S ORIGINAL... ON 73RD STREET!
I'M COMING, CARLITOS!

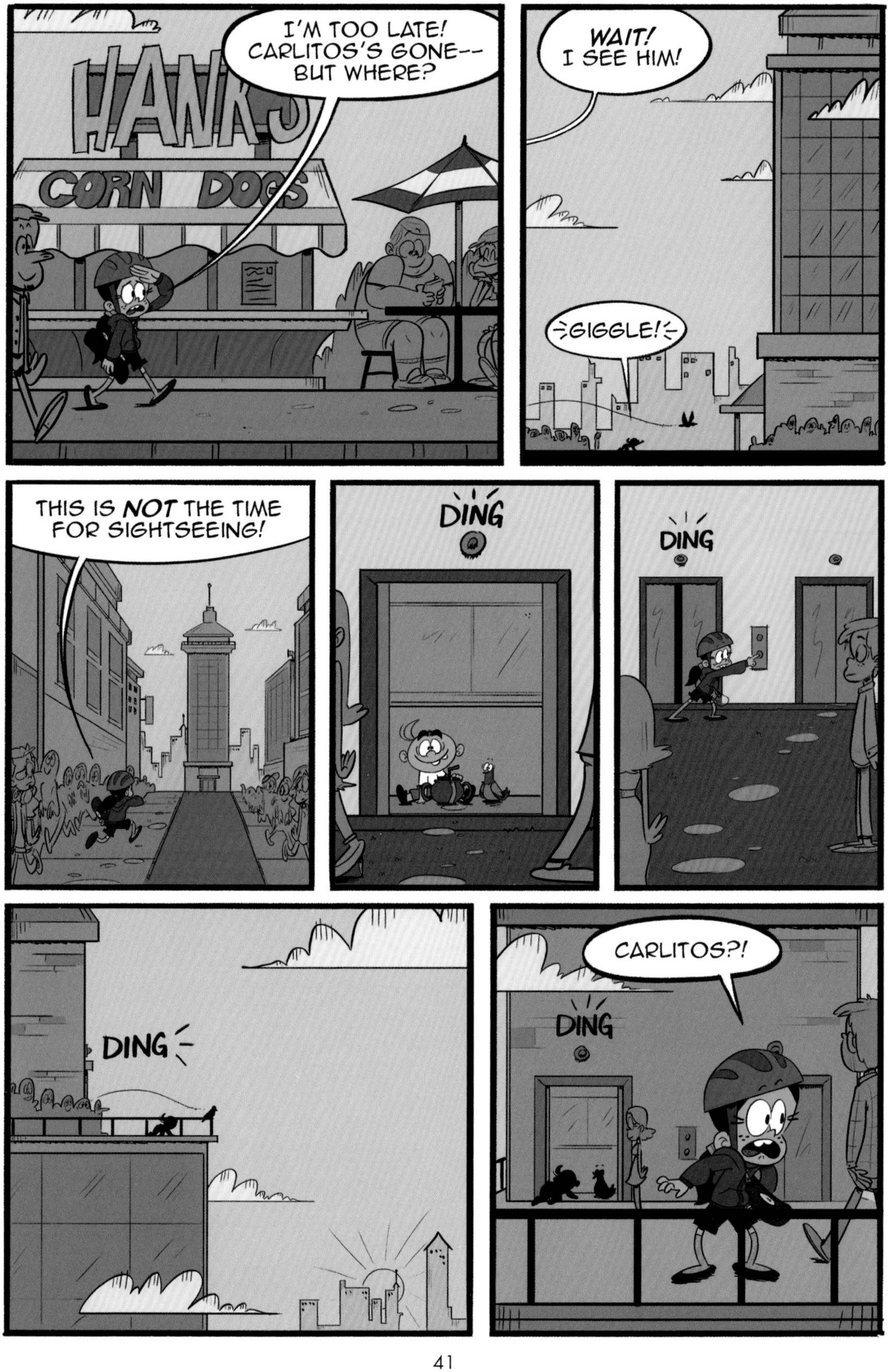
HANK'S
CORN DOGS
I'M TOO LATE! CARLITOS'S GONE-- BUT WHERE?
WAIT! I SEE HIM!
GIGGLE!
THIS IS NOT THE TIME FOR SIGHTSEEING!
DING
DING
DING
CARLITOS?!
DING

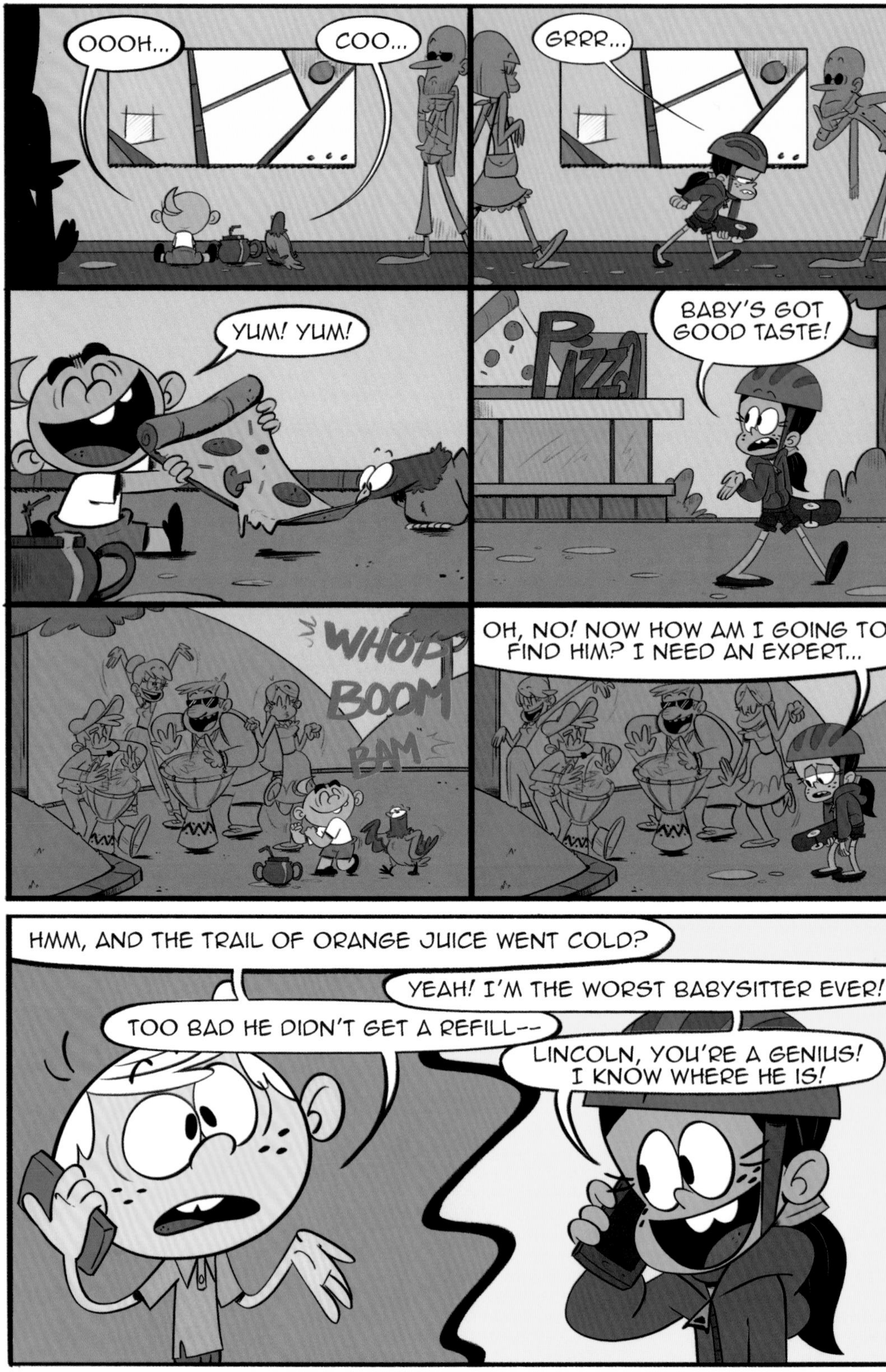
OOOH...
COO...
GRRR...
YUM! YUM!
PIZZA
BABY'S GOT GOOD TASTE!
WHOP
BOOM
BAM
OH, NO! NOW HOW AM I GOING TO FIND HIM? I NEED AN EXPERT...
HMM, AND THE TRAIL OF ORANGE JUICE WENT COLD?
YEAH! I'M THE WORST BABYSITTER EVER!
TOO BAD HE DIDN'T GET A REFILL--
LINCOLN, YOU'RE A GENIUS! I KNOW WHERE HE IS!

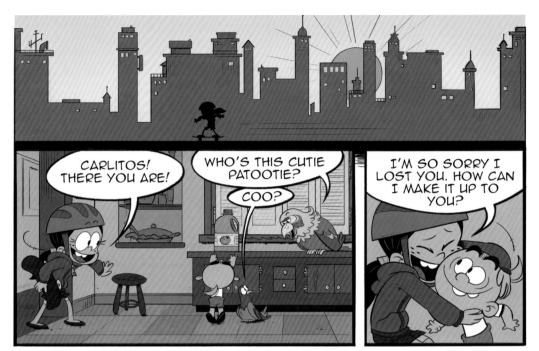

CARLITOS! THERE YOU ARE!

WHO'S THIS CUTIE PATOOTIE?

COO?

I'M SO SORRY I LOST YOU. HOW CAN I MAKE IT UP TO YOU?

HAHA, THAT I CAN DO!

¡MÁS!

HEY, RONNIE ANNE, HOW DID TODAY GO WITH CARLITOS?

OH, I'D SAY IT WAS PRETTY UNEVENTFUL.

UNEVENTFUL?

THAT'S NOT WHAT--

SERGIO, I FORGOT TO TELL YOU... ON THIS NEXT SEASON OF "THE DREAM BOAT", THEY'RE BRINGING BACK ROCKY!

TELL ME MORE...

HEE HEE HEE!

END.

"A PIRATE'S LIFE FOR CJ"

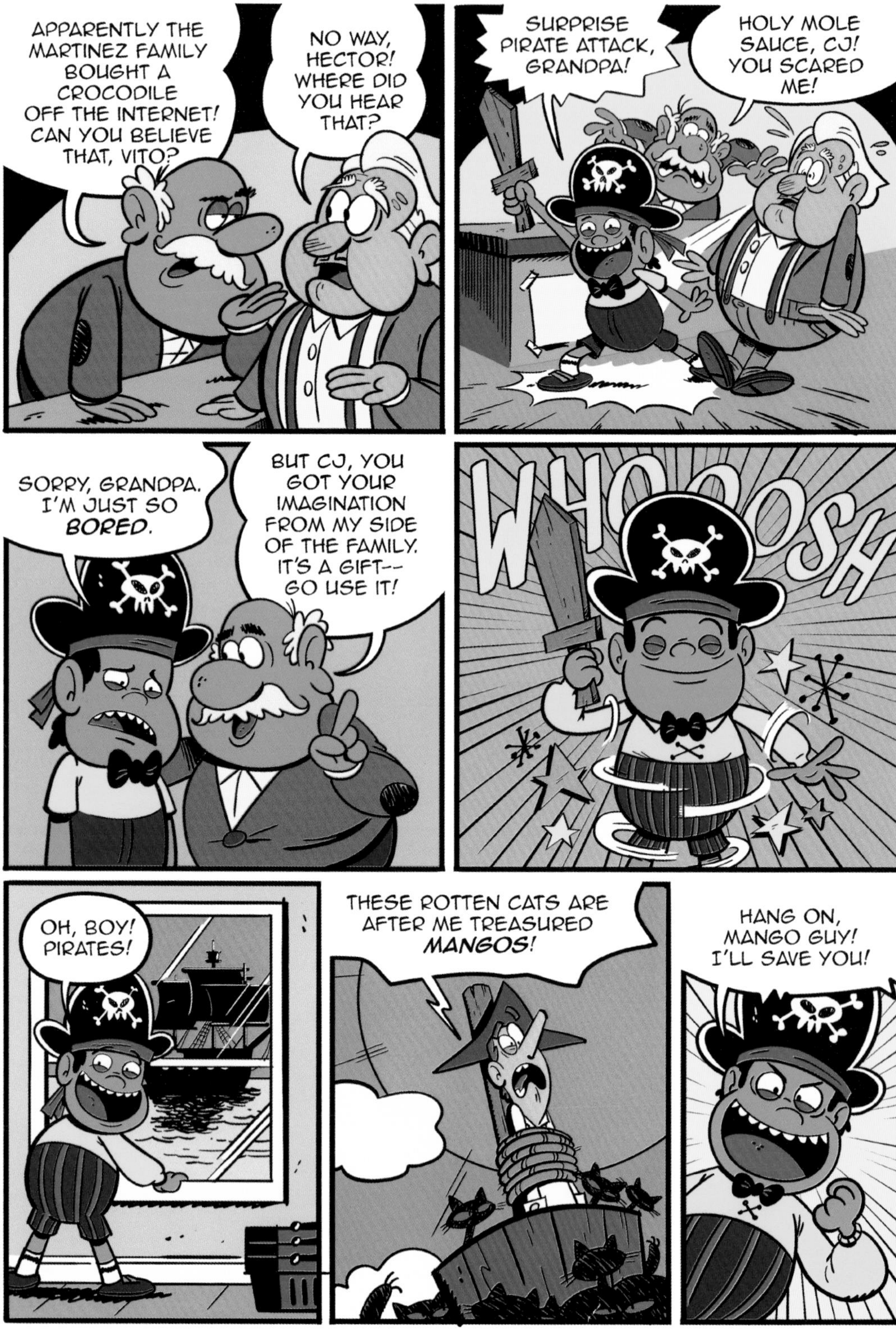
APPARENTLY THE MARTINEZ FAMILY BOUGHT A CROCODILE OFF THE INTERNET! CAN YOU BELIEVE THAT, VITO?
NO WAY, HECTOR! WHERE DID YOU HEAR THAT?
SURPRISE PIRATE ATTACK, GRANDPA!
HOLY MOLE SAUCE, CJ! YOU SCARED ME!
SORRY, GRANDPA. I'M JUST SO ***BORED***.
BUT CJ, YOU GOT YOUR IMAGINATION FROM MY SIDE OF THE FAMILY. IT'S A GIFT-- GO USE IT!
WHOOOSH
OH, BOY! PIRATES!
THESE ROTTEN CATS ARE AFTER ME TREASURED ***MANGOS***!
HANG ON, MANGO GUY! I'LL SAVE YOU!

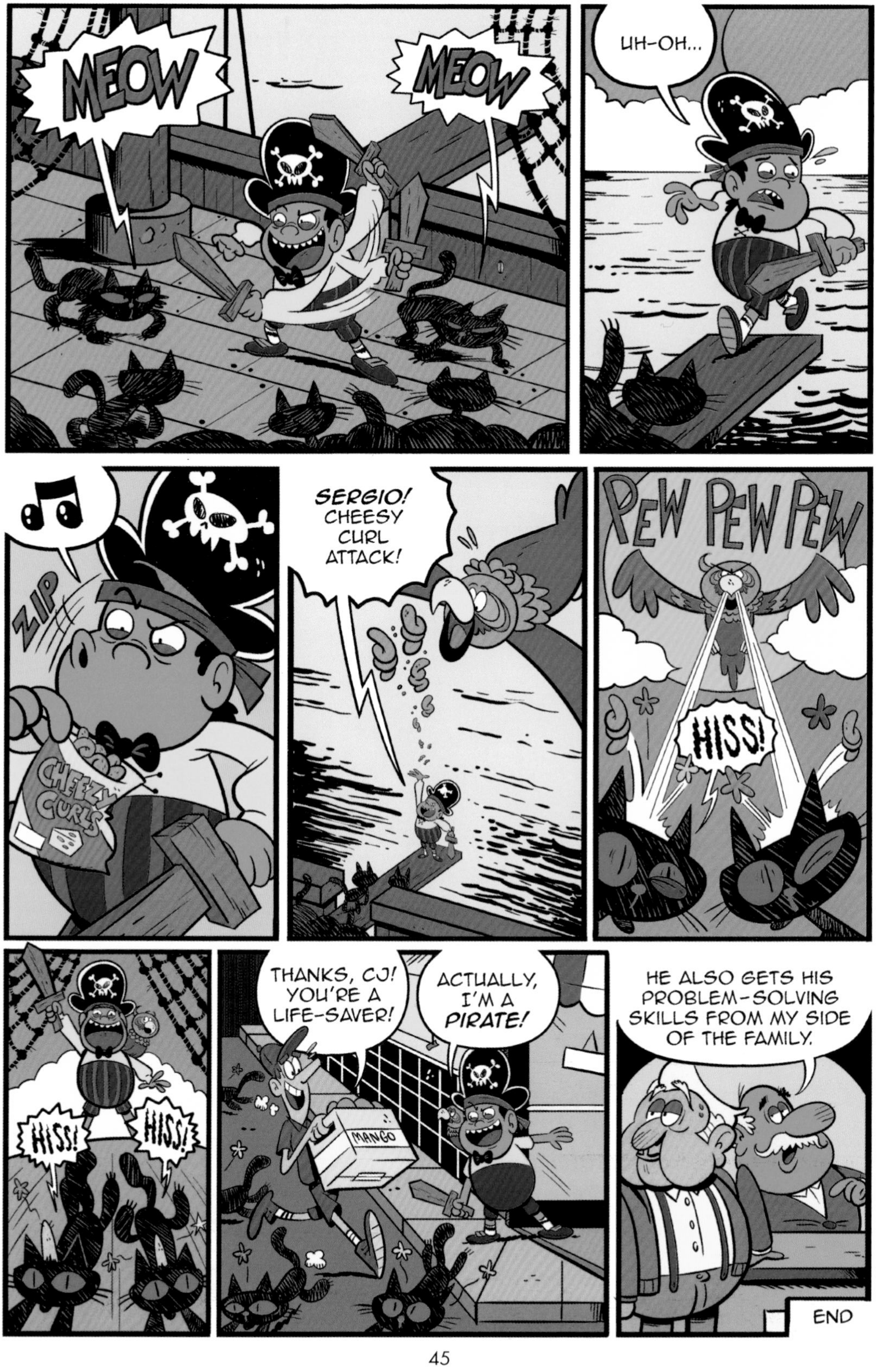
MEOW
MEOW
UH-OH...
ZIP
SERGIO! CHEESY CURL ATTACK!
PEW PEW PEW
HISS!
HISS!
HISS!
THANKS, CJ! YOU'RE A LIFE-SAVER!
ACTUALLY, I'M A PIRATE!
MANGO
HE ALSO GETS HIS PROBLEM-SOLVING SKILLS FROM MY SIDE OF THE FAMILY.
END

"ROCK-A-BYE, CARLITOS"

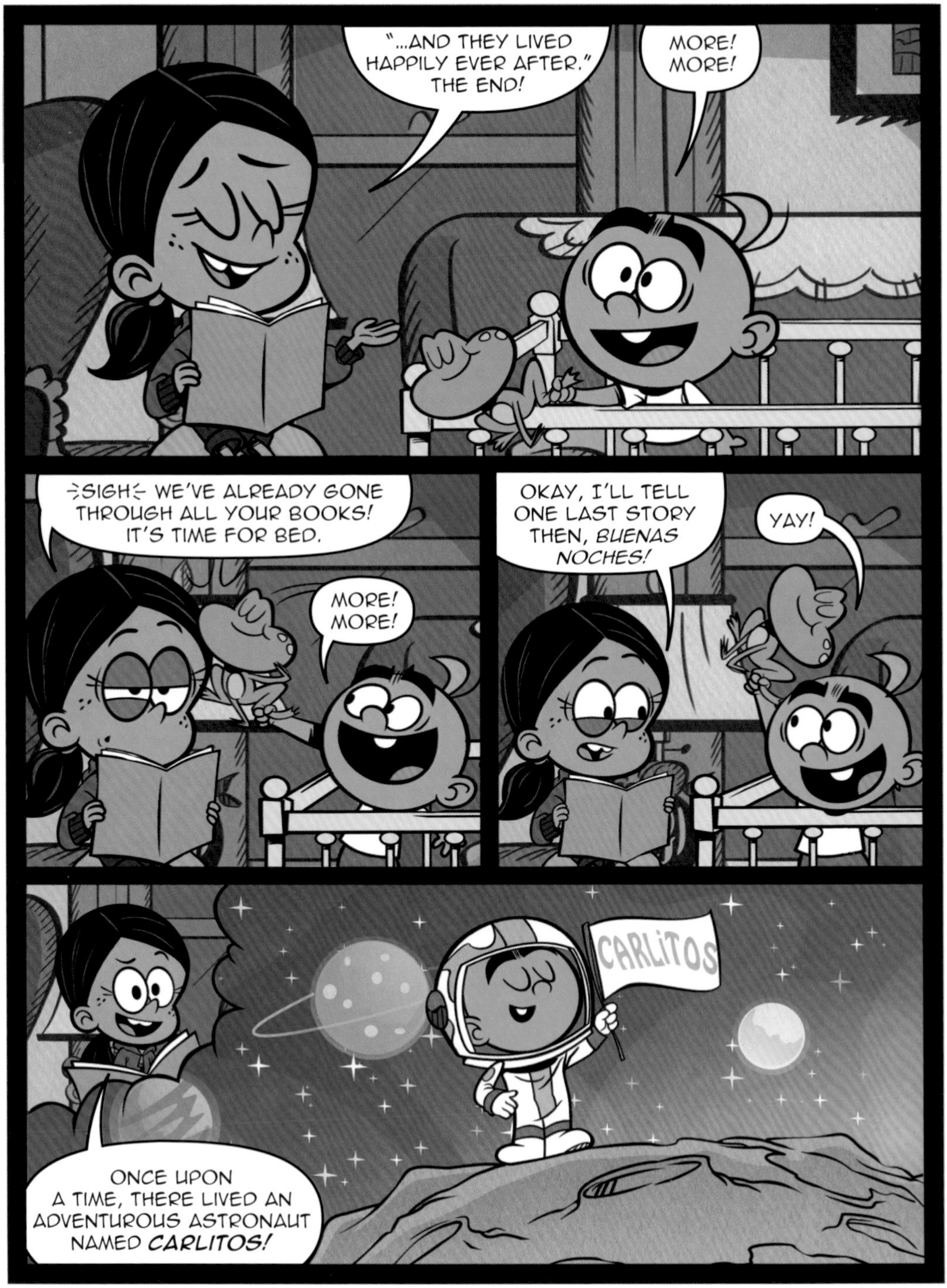

"...AND THEY LIVED HAPPILY EVER AFTER." THE END!
MORE! MORE!
-SIGH- WE'VE ALREADY GONE THROUGH ALL YOUR BOOKS! IT'S TIME FOR BED.
MORE! MORE!
OKAY, I'LL TELL ONE LAST STORY THEN, *BUENAS NOCHES!*
YAY!
CARLITOS
ONCE UPON A TIME, THERE LIVED AN ADVENTUROUS ASTRONAUT NAMED *CARLITOS!*

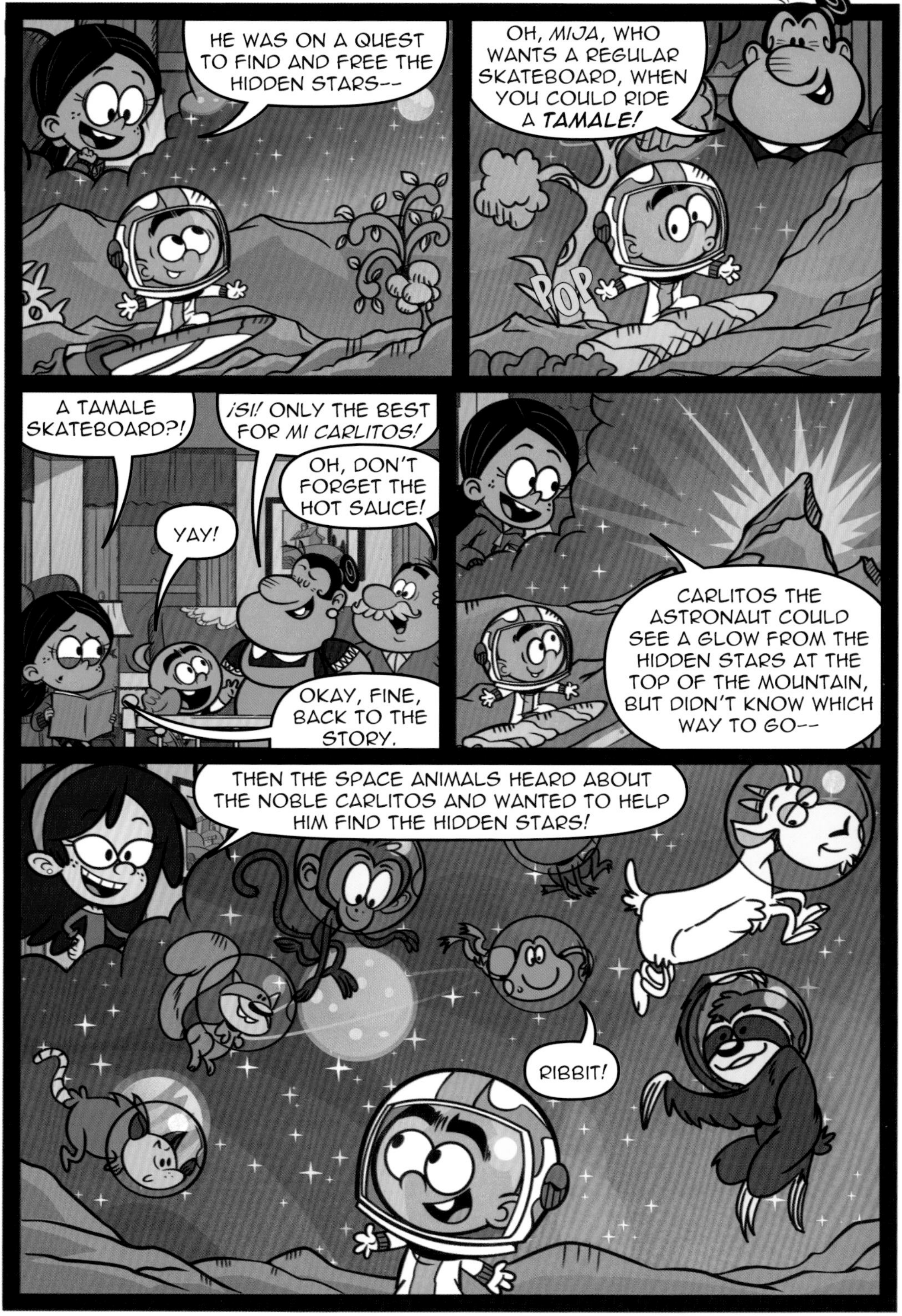
HE WAS ON A QUEST TO FIND AND FREE THE HIDDEN STARS--
OH, *MIJA*, WHO WANTS A REGULAR SKATEBOARD, WHEN YOU COULD RIDE A ***TAMALE!***
POP
A TAMALE SKATEBOARD?!
¡SI! ONLY THE BEST FOR *MI CARLITOS!*
OH, DON'T FORGET THE HOT SAUCE!
YAY!
OKAY, FINE, BACK TO THE STORY.
CARLITOS THE ASTRONAUT COULD SEE A GLOW FROM THE HIDDEN STARS AT THE TOP OF THE MOUNTAIN, BUT DIDN'T KNOW WHICH WAY TO GO--
THEN THE SPACE ANIMALS HEARD ABOUT THE NOBLE CARLITOS AND WANTED TO HELP HIM FIND THE HIDDEN STARS!
RIBBIT!

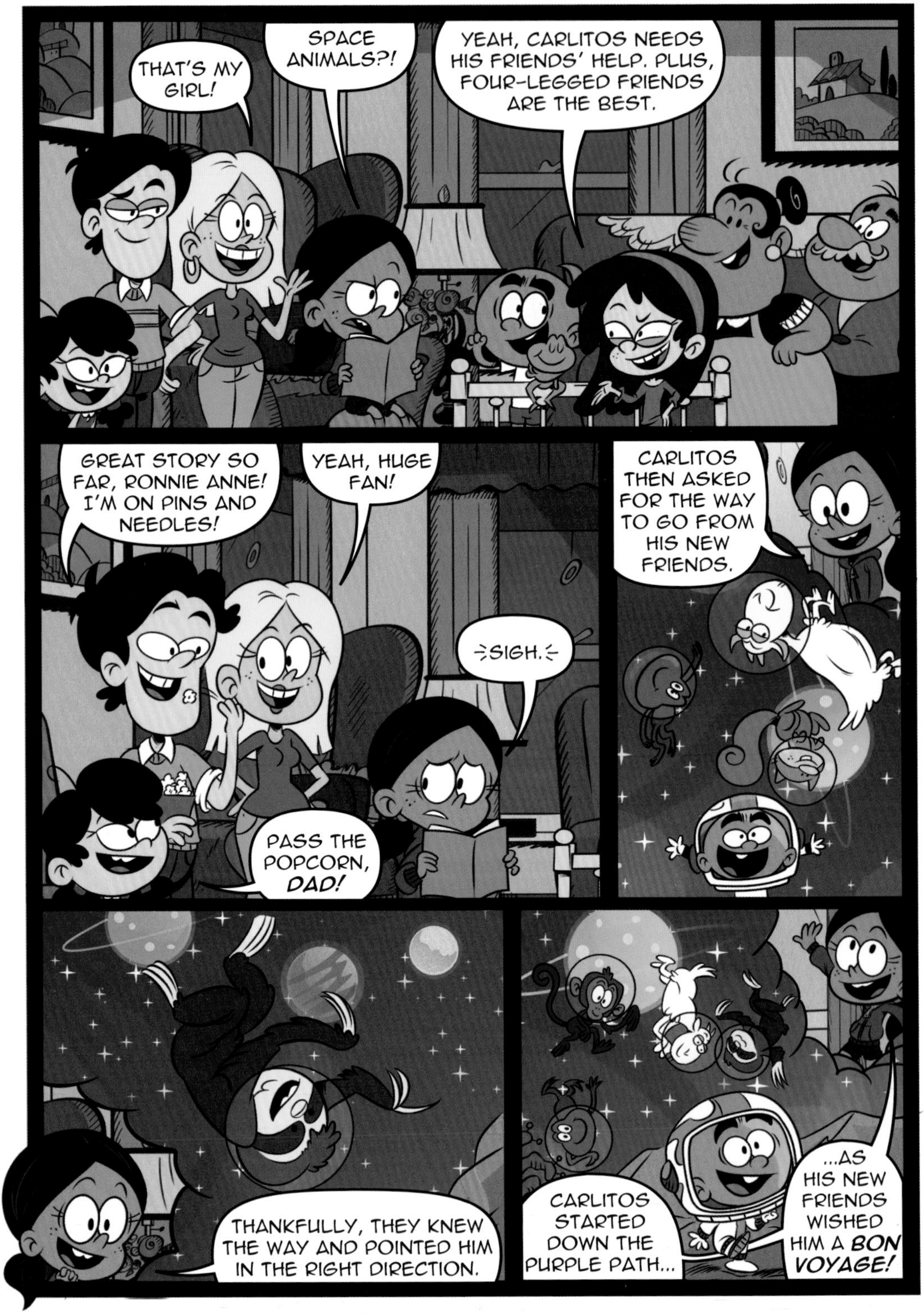
THAT'S MY GIRL!
SPACE ANIMALS?!
YEAH, CARLITOS NEEDS HIS FRIENDS' HELP. PLUS, FOUR-LEGGED FRIENDS ARE THE BEST.
GREAT STORY SO FAR, RONNIE ANNE! I'M ON PINS AND NEEDLES!
YEAH, HUGE FAN!
-SIGH.-
PASS THE POPCORN, *DAD!*
CARLITOS THEN ASKED FOR THE WAY TO GO FROM HIS NEW FRIENDS.
THANKFULLY, THEY KNEW THE WAY AND POINTED HIM IN THE RIGHT DIRECTION.
CARLITOS STARTED DOWN THE PURPLE PATH...
...AS HIS NEW FRIENDS WISHED HIM A *BON VOYAGE!*

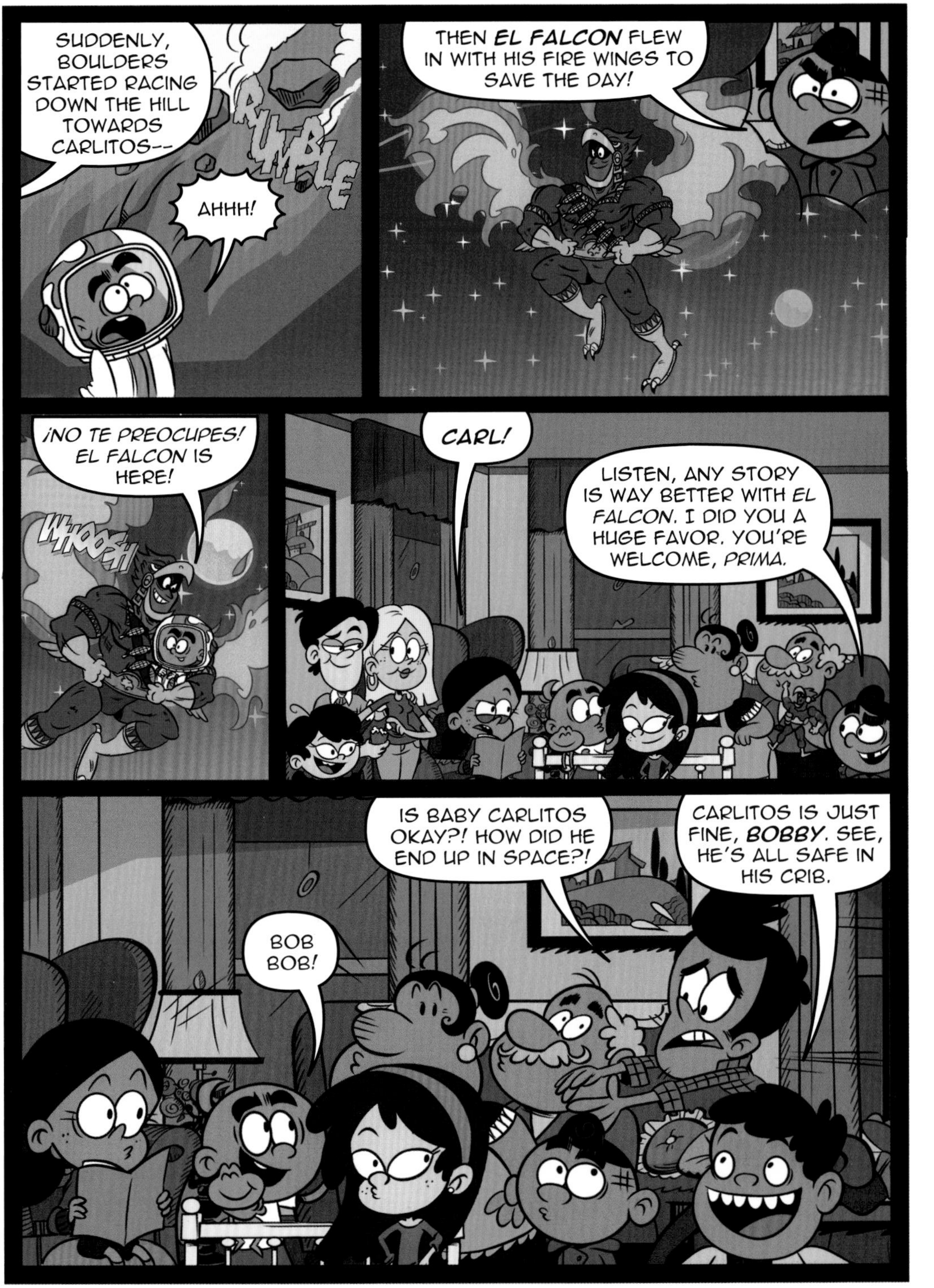
SUDDENLY, BOULDERS STARTED RACING DOWN THE HILL TOWARDS CARLITOS--
RUMBLE
AHHH!
THEN EL FALCON FLEW IN WITH HIS FIRE WINGS TO SAVE THE DAY!
¡NO TE PREOCUPES! EL FALCON IS HERE!
WHOOSH
CARL!
LISTEN, ANY STORY IS WAY BETTER WITH EL FALCON. I DID YOU A HUGE FAVOR. YOU'RE WELCOME, PRIMA.
BOB BOB!
IS BABY CARLITOS OKAY?! HOW DID HE END UP IN SPACE?!
CARLITOS IS JUST FINE, BOBBY. SEE, HE'S ALL SAFE IN HIS CRIB.

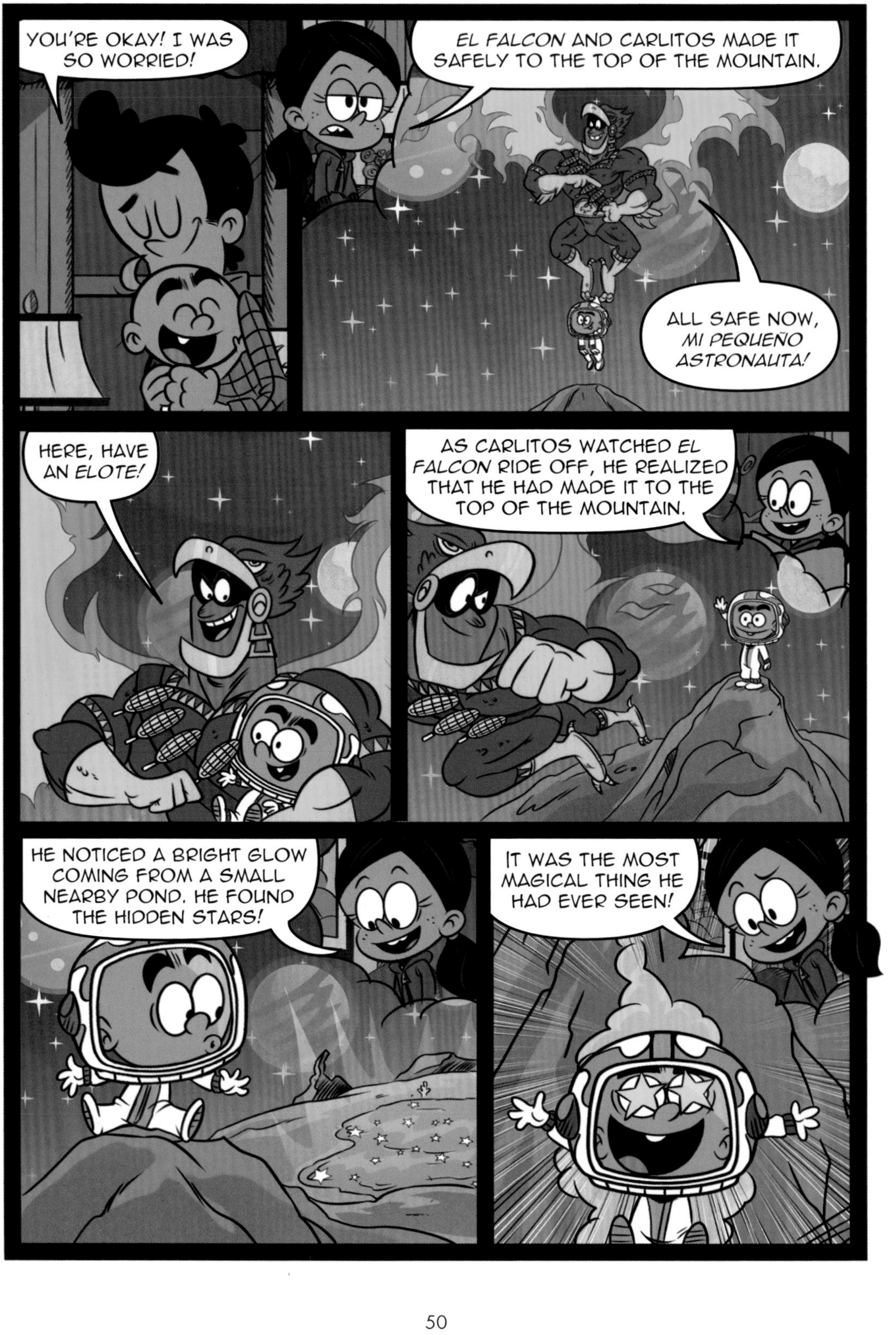
YOU'RE OKAY! I WAS SO WORRIED!
EL FALCON AND CARLITOS MADE IT SAFELY TO THE TOP OF THE MOUNTAIN.
ALL SAFE NOW, *MI PEQUEÑO ASTRONAUTA!*
HERE, HAVE AN *ELOTE!*
AS CARLITOS WATCHED *EL FALCON* RIDE OFF, HE REALIZED THAT HE HAD MADE IT TO THE TOP OF THE MOUNTAIN.
HE NOTICED A BRIGHT GLOW COMING FROM A SMALL NEARBY POND. HE FOUND THE HIDDEN STARS!
IT WAS THE MOST MAGICAL THING HE HAD EVER SEEN!

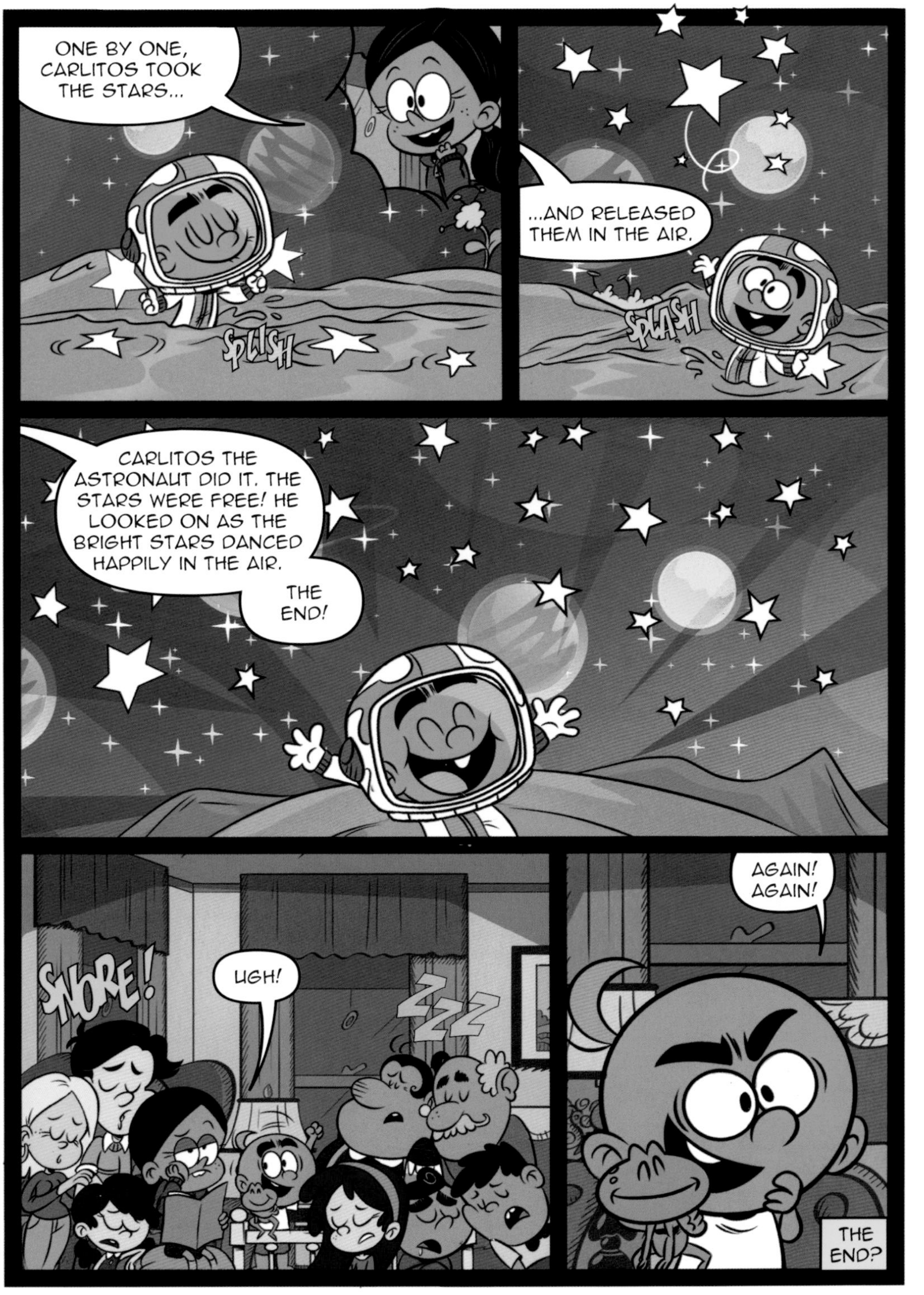
ONE BY ONE, CARLITOS TOOK THE STARS...
SPLISH
...AND RELEASED THEM IN THE AIR.
SPLASH
CARLITOS THE ASTRONAUT DID IT. THE STARS WERE FREE! HE LOOKED ON AS THE BRIGHT STARS DANCED HAPPILY IN THE AIR.
THE END!
SNORE!
UGH!
ZZZ
AGAIN! AGAIN!
THE END?

"SLEDDIN' THE GNAR"

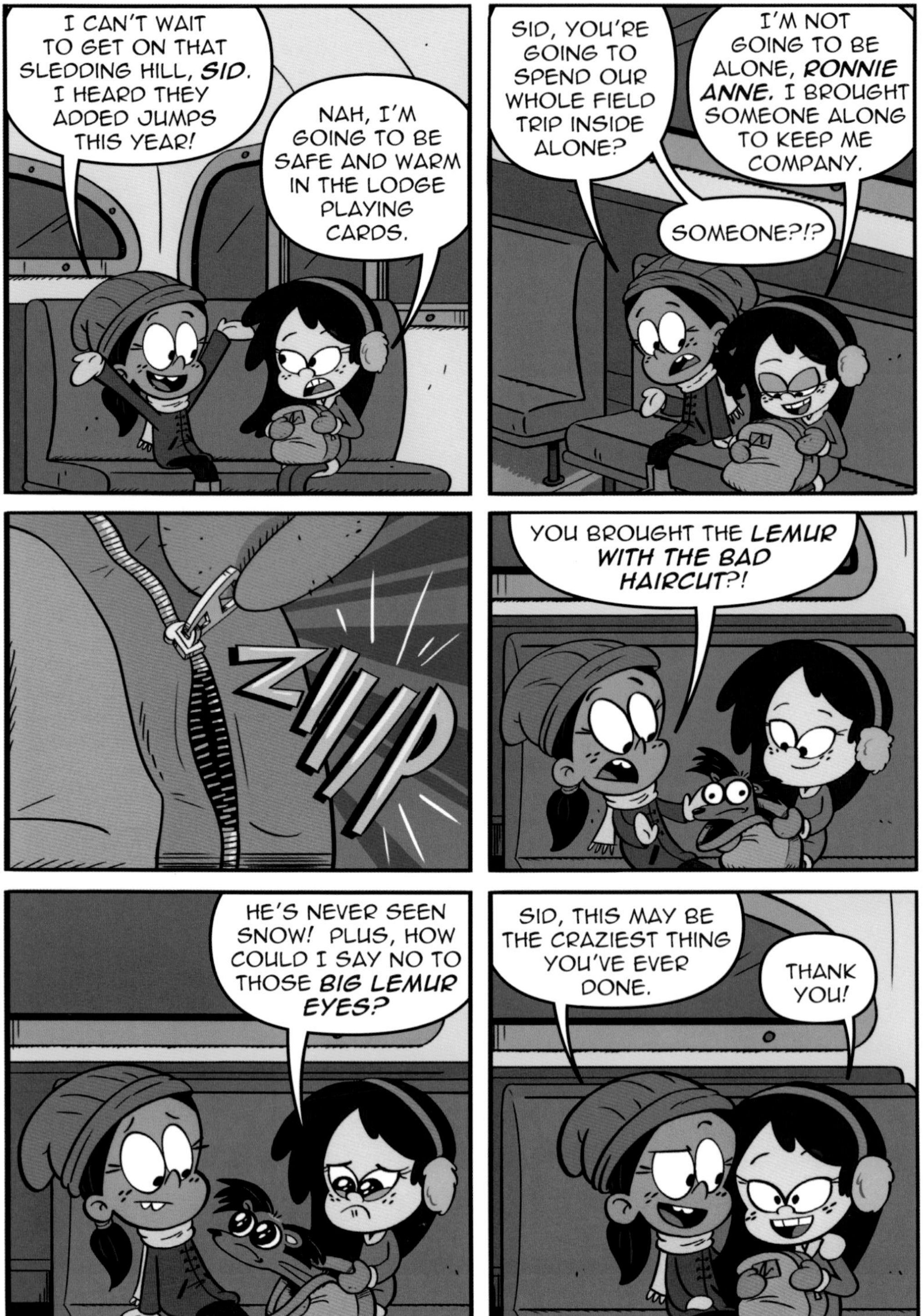
I CAN'T WAIT TO GET ON THAT SLEDDING HILL, *SID*. I HEARD THEY ADDED JUMPS THIS YEAR!
NAH, I'M GOING TO BE SAFE AND WARM IN THE LODGE PLAYING CARDS.
SID, YOU'RE GOING TO SPEND OUR WHOLE FIELD TRIP INSIDE ALONE?
I'M NOT GOING TO BE ALONE, *RONNIE ANNE.* I BROUGHT SOMEONE ALONG TO KEEP ME COMPANY.
SOMEONE?!?
ZIIIP
YOU BROUGHT THE *LEMUR WITH THE BAD HAIRCUT*?!
HE'S NEVER SEEN SNOW! PLUS, HOW COULD I SAY NO TO THOSE *BIG LEMUR EYES?*
SID, THIS MAY BE THE CRAZIEST THING YOU'VE EVER DONE.
THANK YOU!

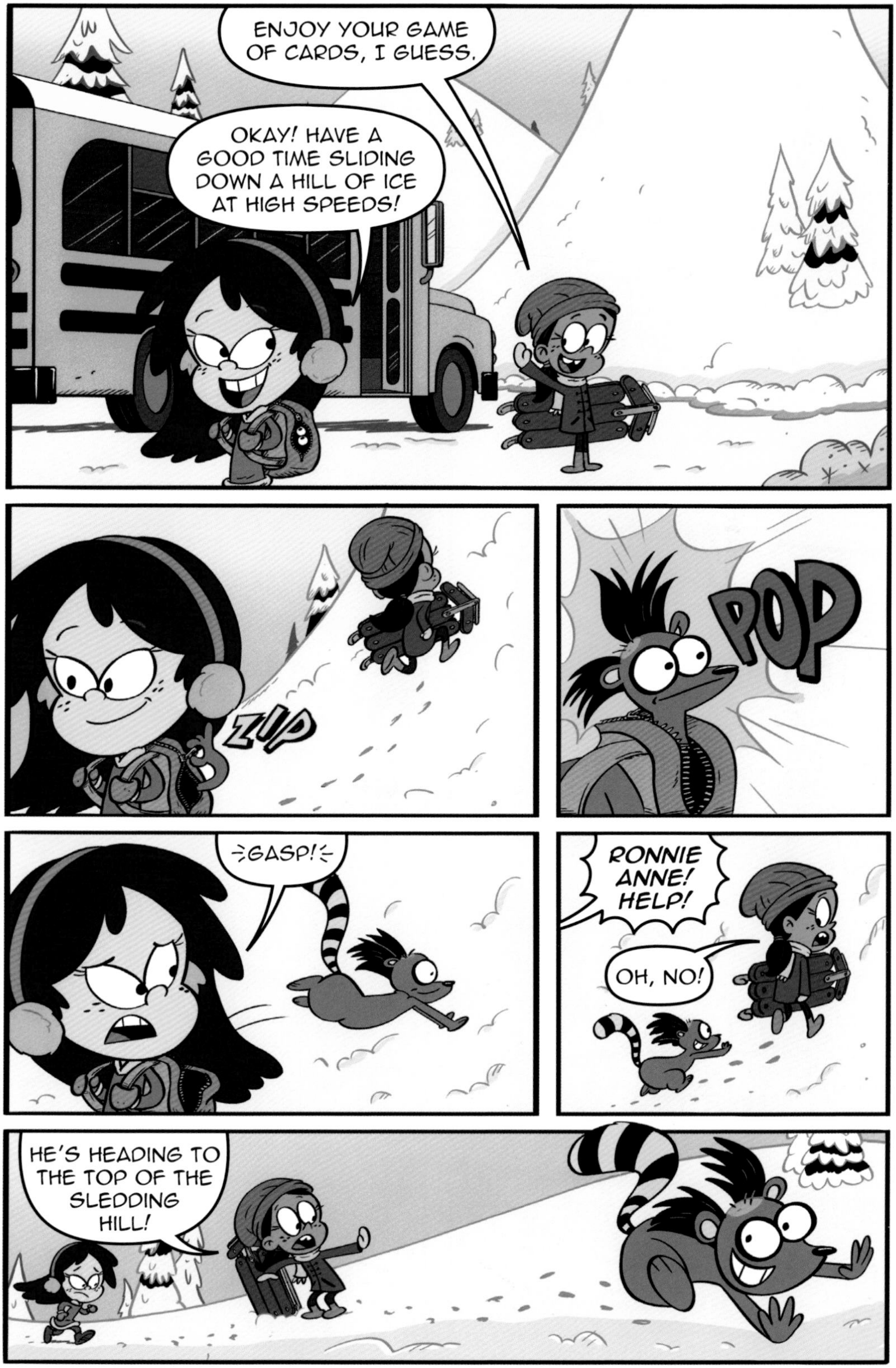
ENJOY YOUR GAME OF CARDS, I GUESS.
OKAY! HAVE A GOOD TIME SLIDING DOWN A HILL OF ICE AT HIGH SPEEDS!
ZIP
POP
GASP!
RONNIE ANNE! HELP!
OH, NO!
HE'S HEADING TO THE TOP OF THE SLEDDING HILL!

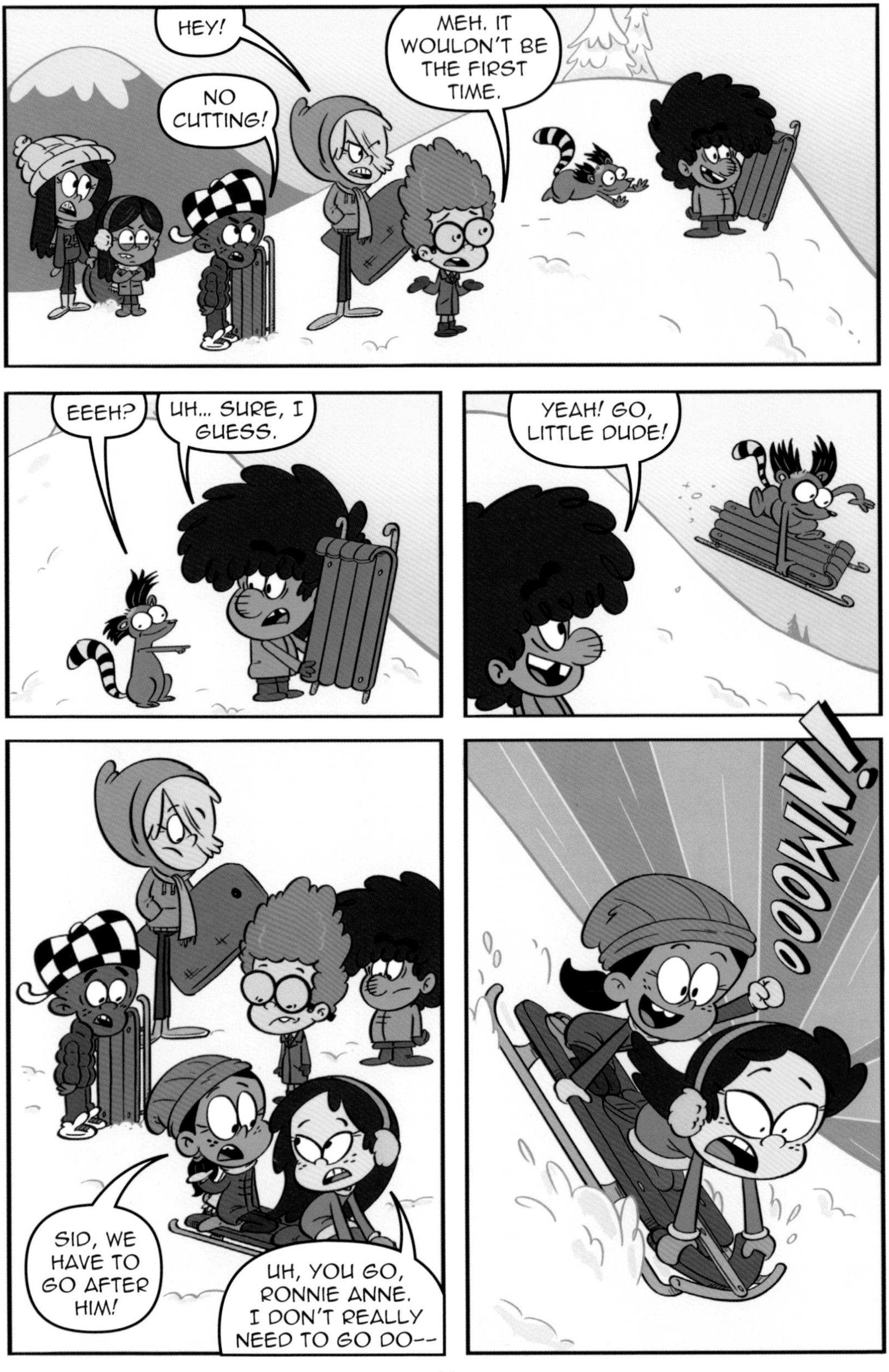
HEY!
NO CUTTING!
MEH. IT WOULDN'T BE THE FIRST TIME.
EEEH?
UH... SURE, I GUESS.
YEAH! GO, LITTLE DUDE!
SID, WE HAVE TO GO AFTER HIM!
UH, YOU GO, RONNIE ANNE. I DON'T REALLY NEED TO GO DO--
WOOOOOM!

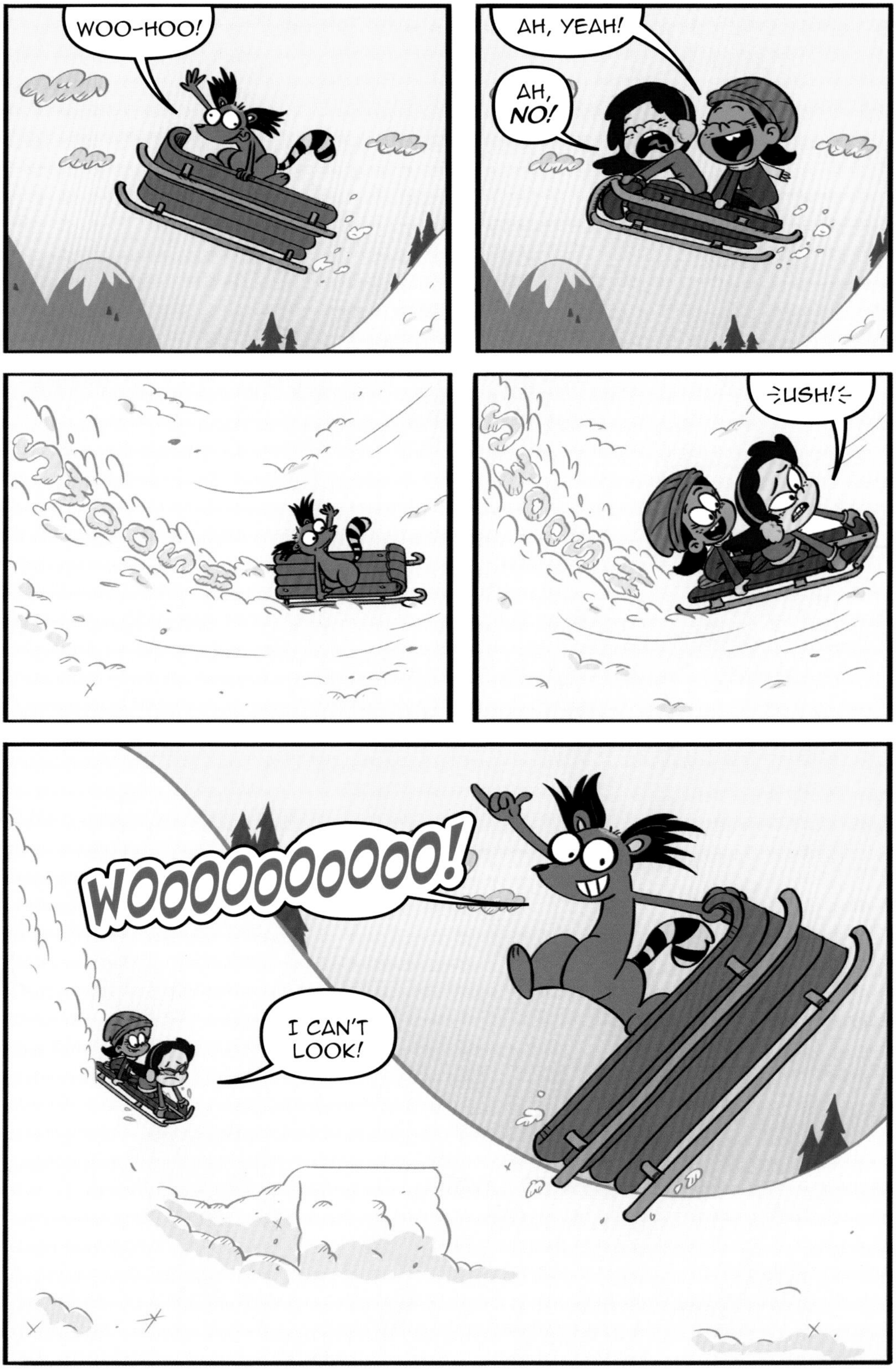
WOO-HOO!
AH, YEAH!
AH, NO!
USH!
WOOOOOOOOOO!
I CAN'T LOOK!

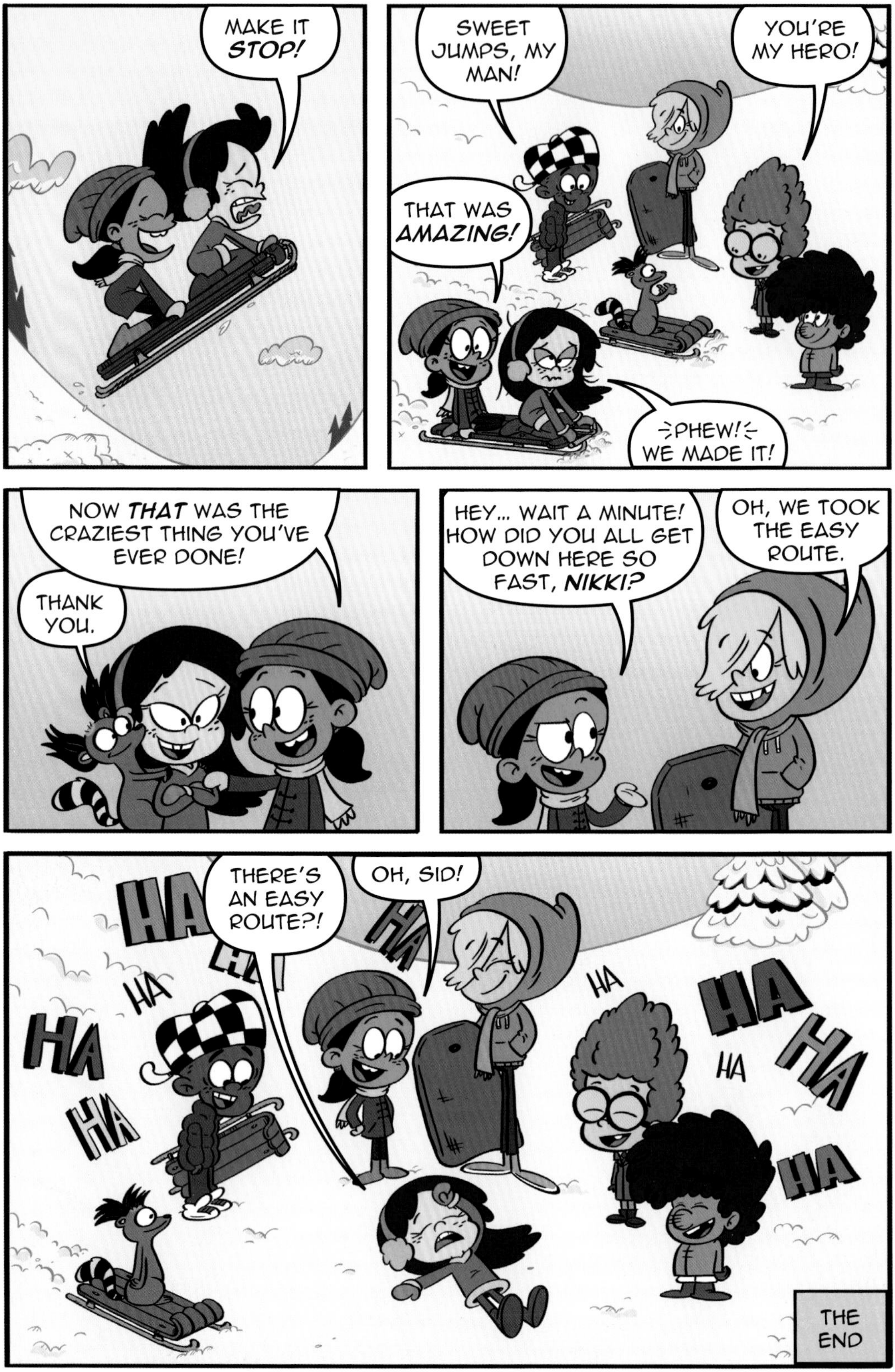
MAKE IT STOP!
SWEET JUMPS, MY MAN!
YOU'RE MY HERO!
THAT WAS AMAZING!
PHEW! WE MADE IT!
NOW THAT WAS THE CRAZIEST THING YOU'VE EVER DONE!
THANK YOU.
HEY... WAIT A MINUTE! HOW DID YOU ALL GET DOWN HERE SO FAST, NIKKI?
OH, WE TOOK THE EASY ROUTE.
THERE'S AN EASY ROUTE?!
OH, SID!
HA HA HA HA HA HA HA HA HA HA HA HA
THE END

"FOR A FEW TICKETS MORE"

WAITAMINUTE!

PRIZES!

OOOOOH!

30,000   10

SKREECH

★ COLLECTIBLE FIGURE ★
SUPER RARE
MUSCLE FISH!
FOR THE ULTIMATE MUSCLE FISH FAN

MUSCLE FISH BOX

Muscle Fish Doll
30,000 TICKETS

OH, SOBRINA, IT'S OKAY THEY ALWAYS MAKE THOSE PRIZES TOO EXPENSIVE ON PURPOSE.

FOR THE ULTIMATE MUSCLE FISH FAN

Muscle Fish Doll
30,000 TICKETS

WHOA.

INDEED. 30,000 TICKETS WOULD REQUIRE THE EFFORT OF SOME SORT OF TEAM, A SINGLE PERSON COULDN'T POSSIBLY GATHER THAT QUANTITY.

IT'S TOO MUCH!

HMM...A TEAM, EH?

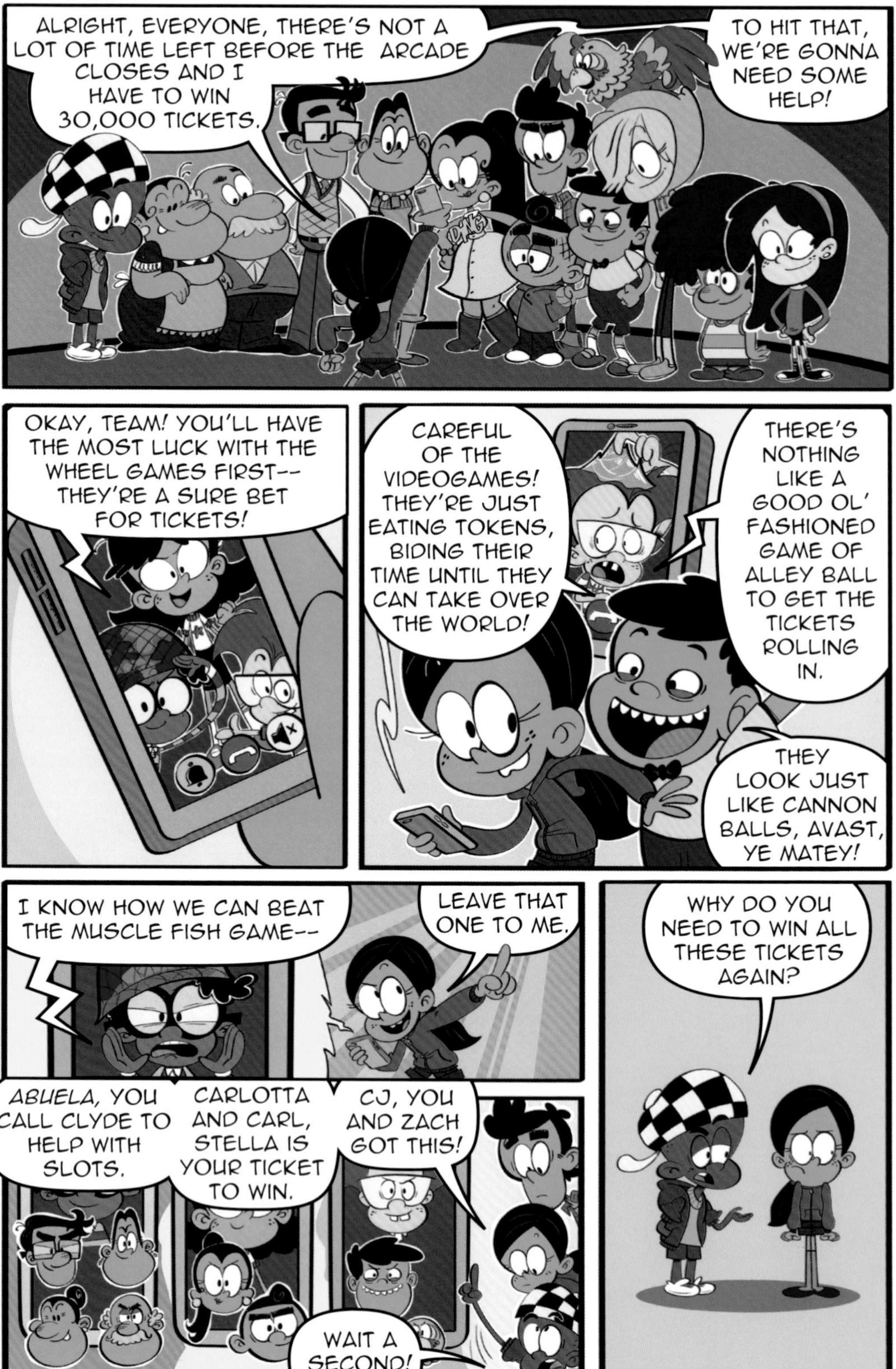
ALRIGHT, EVERYONE, THERE'S NOT A LOT OF TIME LEFT BEFORE THE ARCADE CLOSES AND I HAVE TO WIN 30,000 TICKETS.
TO HIT THAT, WE'RE GONNA NEED SOME HELP!
OKAY, TEAM! YOU'LL HAVE THE MOST LUCK WITH THE WHEEL GAMES FIRST-- THEY'RE A SURE BET FOR TICKETS!
CAREFUL OF THE VIDEOGAMES! THEY'RE JUST EATING TOKENS, BIDING THEIR TIME UNTIL THEY CAN TAKE OVER THE WORLD!
THERE'S NOTHING LIKE A GOOD OL' FASHIONED GAME OF ALLEY BALL TO GET THE TICKETS ROLLING IN.
THEY LOOK JUST LIKE CANNON BALLS, AVAST, YE MATEY!
I KNOW HOW WE CAN BEAT THE MUSCLE FISH GAME--
LEAVE THAT ONE TO ME.
ABUELA, YOU CALL CLYDE TO HELP WITH SLOTS.
CARLOTTA AND CARL, STELLA IS YOUR TICKET TO WIN.
CJ, YOU AND ZACH GOT THIS!
WAIT A SECOND!
WHY DO YOU NEED TO WIN ALL THESE TICKETS AGAIN?

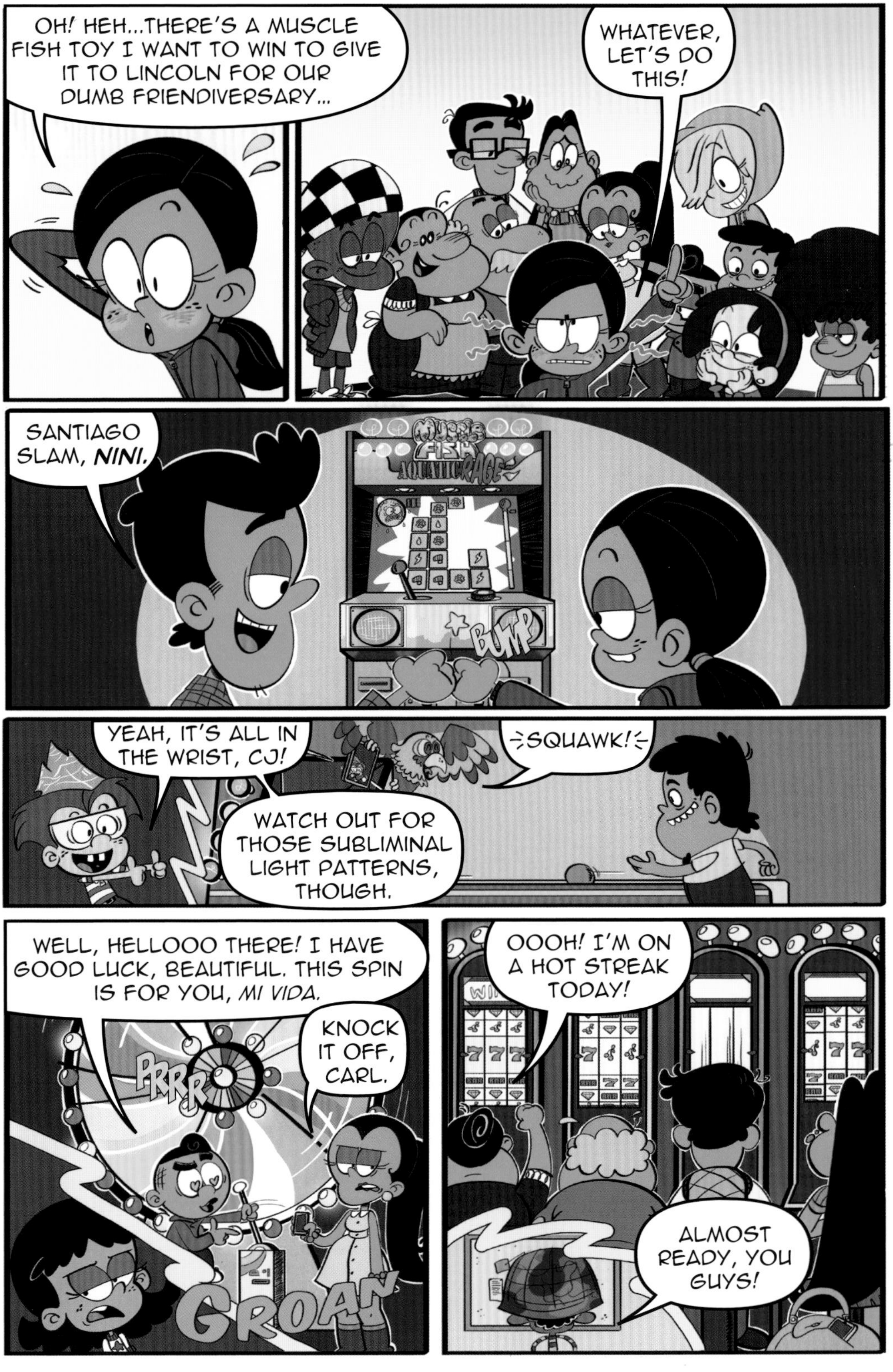
OH! HEH...THERE'S A MUSCLE FISH TOY I WANT TO WIN TO GIVE IT TO LINCOLN FOR OUR DUMB FRIENDIVERSARY...
WHATEVER, LET'S DO THIS!
SANTIAGO SLAM, **NINI.**
MUSCLE FISH AQUATIC RAGE
BUMP
YEAH, IT'S ALL IN THE WRIST, CJ!
SQUAWK!
WATCH OUT FOR THOSE SUBLIMINAL LIGHT PATTERNS, THOUGH.
WELL, HELLOOO THERE! I HAVE GOOD LUCK, BEAUTIFUL. THIS SPIN IS FOR YOU, *MI VIDA.*
KNOCK IT OFF, CARL.
PRRR
GROAN
OOOH! I'M ON A HOT STREAK TODAY!
ALMOST READY, YOU GUYS!

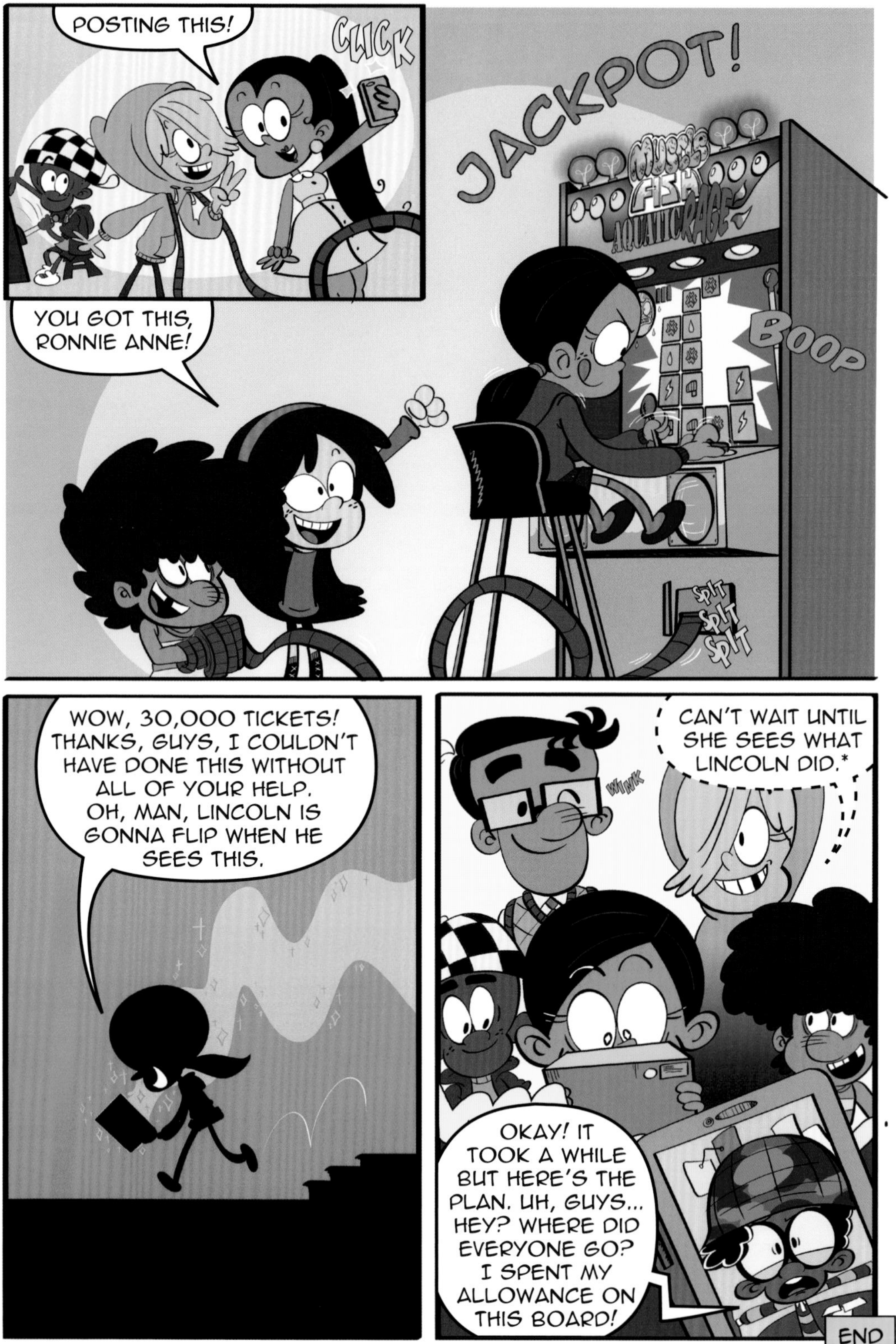
POSTING THIS!
CLICK
YOU GOT THIS, RONNIE ANNE!
JACKPOT!
BOOP
SPIT
SPIT
SPIT
WOW, 30,000 TICKETS! THANKS, GUYS, I COULDN'T HAVE DONE THIS WITHOUT ALL OF YOUR HELP. OH, MAN, LINCOLN IS GONNA FLIP WHEN HE SEES THIS.
WINK
CAN'T WAIT UNTIL SHE SEES WHAT LINCOLN DID.*
OKAY! IT TOOK A WHILE BUT HERE'S THE PLAN. UH, GUYS... HEY? WHERE DID EVERYONE GO? I SPENT MY ALLOWANCE ON THIS BOARD!
END

*SEE "OLLIE OLLIE OXEN FREE" IN THE LOUD HOUSE #12 "THE CASE OF THE STOLEN DRAWERS" FOR LINCOLN'S SURPRISE FOR RONNIE ANNE!

WATCH OUT FOR PAPERCUTZ

¡Hola! Welcome to the very first graphic novel about THE CASAGRANDES, the top-rated animated show spinning off from THE LOUD HOUSE that's all about the culture, humor and love of growing up in a multi-generational Mexican-American family... It's brought to you by Papercutz, those bilingual folks dedicated to publishing great graphic novels for all ages. I'm Jim Salicrup, Editor-in-Chief and something else I've rarely talked about in public—I'm half Spanish. Technically I'm a quarter Spanish, and a quarter Puerto Rican, but I'm still excited to see Latinx culture so wonderfully represented in graphic novels.

But the really exciting news was just announced: Nickelodeon, the number-one network for kids, has greenlit a third season of *The Casagrandes*, which will find Ronnie Anne and her family members on a variety of adventures while exploring different areas of the city. A spinoff of Nickelodeon's top-rated animated series *The Loud House*, Emmy Award-winning *The Casagrandes* has ranked as the number two animated property across television with Kids 2-11 since its Oct. 2019 debut. Season three is currently in production by Nickelodeon Animation Studio.

"Our audience has loved the diverse characters, relatable stories, and rich animation found in *The Casagrandes* since the series debuted," said Ramsey Naito, President, Nickelodeon Animation. "The success of the show is due to the creative leadership who continue to showcase the love and laughter of this family, living in an environment that reflects the global world we live in today."

The new season will feature a variety of guest stars giving voice to new and returning characters, including Danny Trejo (*Spy Kids*), pop star Ally Brooke, Jorge Gutierrez (*The Book of Life*), Stephanie Beatriz (*Brooklyn Nine-Nine*), Justin Chon (*Twilight*) and more.

The Casagrandes voice cast includes: Izabella Alvarez (*Westworld*) as Ronnie Anne; Carlos PenaVega (*Big Time Rush*) as Bobby; Eugenio Derbez (*Dora and the Lost City of Gold*) as Arturo; Carlos Alazraqui (*The Fairly OddParents*) as Carlos, "Tio;" Roxana Ortega (The League) as Frida, "Tia;" Alexa PenaVega (*Spy Kids*) as Carlota; Jared Kozak (*Born this Way*) as CJ; Alex Cazares (*The Boss Baby: Back in Business*) as Carl; Ruben Garfias (*East Los High*) as Hector, "Abuelo;" Sonia Manzano (*Sesame Street*) as Rosa, "Abuela." Additionally, Ken Jeong (*Dr. Ken*) gives voice as Stanley; Melissa Joan Hart (*Sabrina the Teenage Witch*) as Becca; Leah Mei Gold (*Legion*) as Sid; and Lexi Sexton (*The Loud House*) as Adelaide.

Emmy Award-winning *The Casagrandes* is executive produced by Michael Rubiner. Miguel Puga serves as co-executive producer, Alan Foreman is supervising producer and Miguel Gonzalez serves as art director, with award-winning cartoonist Lalo Alcaraz as consulting producer and cultural consultant.

As a special added bonus for this premiere volume of THE CASAGRANDES, we're featuring three exclusive mini-interviews with a few of the real live talents behind the Nickelodeon show. On the following pages you'll get to meet Co-Executive Producer Miguel Puga, Consulting Producer and Cultural Consultant Lalo Alcaraz, and the voice of Ronnie Anne, Izabella Alvarez. I was thrilled to have the opportunity to ask them questions which they so generously took the time to answer.

And if that wasn't enough, we've saved another bit of news for last—another THE CASAGRANDES graphic novel is coming in 2022! If that seems way too long to wait, don't worry, the Casagrande family and friends will continue to pop up in THE LOUD HOUSE graphic novels throughout the year, and of course, continue to star in their show on Nickelodeon. What more could you possibly ask for?

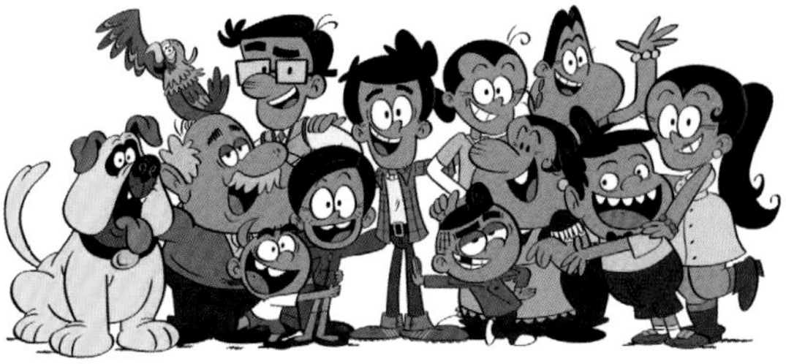

Gracias,

Jim

STAY IN TOUCH!

EMAIL:	salicrup@papercutz.com
WEB:	papercutz.com
TWITTER:	@papercutzgn
INSTAGRAM:	@papercutzgn
FACEBOOK:	PAPERCUTZGRAPHICNOVELS
FANMAIL:	Papercutz, 160 Broadway, Suite 700, East Wing, New York, NY 10038

Go to papercutz.com and sign up for the free Papercutz e-newsletter!

BONUS: BEHIND-THE-SCENES INTERVIEWS

MIGUEL PUGA
Co-Executive Producer

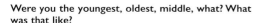

Where/when were you born?

I was born July 3, 1984 in beautiful, sunny, Los Angeles, California.

Was it a large family?

I only had two older brothers. But we were always surrounded by family every day…so yes it was a large, happy family.

Were you the youngest, oldest, middle, what? What was that like?

I was the youngest. My oldest brother is 20 years older than I am, so my parents had me and my middle brother at the age of 50. It was like growing up in a multigenerational family. My parents didn't speak English well, so they only spoke Spanish to us. My first language was Spanish, I didn't start learning English until I was 5-years-old. Thanks to cartoons and television. Being the youngest was a blast. I got away with a lot of things. I was quite mischievous, kind of like Carl Casagrande, and I could act my way out of getting in trouble…like 10% of the time.

In what ways was your family similar to the Casagrandes?

A lot! The Casagrandes are loosely based off of my own family members. Rosa (Abuela) is based off of my mom and my grandmother. Both love to cook and would come up with all kinds of remedies and concoctions for any little thing, including passing a test. Everyone from my older female cousins who helped inspired Carlota, to the living room they live in that was inspired by my own home growing up. I can go on….

In what ways were they different?

We never lived in an apartment in the city. We lived in a house with two units on the lot that felt like we lived in an apartment. We also never owned a *mercado*.

What were your interests growing up?

Comicbooks, toys, drawing, and cartoons, in no particular order. You sit me down in a room with a piece of paper and a pencil and childhood wonder…I would be in there for hours. Never lose that wonder, kids!

What were you favorite cartoons?

I loved *Rocko's Modern Life* and *Batman: The Animated Series*.

Who are your greatest influences? Which cartoons and/or animators inspired you most?

There are so many to list, Walt Disney, Bill Melendez, Sergio Aragonés, Genndy Tartakovsky, Jack Kirby, and John Romita Sr. to name a few. The cartoon that really inspired me the most, hands down has to be *Samurai Jack*. I was in a crossroads after graduating high school, not knowing what to do with my career, until I saw the very first episode of *Samurai Jack* premiere, and right then I knew animation was for me. I always loved drawing, and I knew I wanted to work as an artist, but that cartoon drove me and inspired me to never give up on my dreams. Thanks, Genndy.

What's your average work day like?

Every day is different. But usually in the mornings, I start my day with coffee and a few warm up drawings. I hop in with the writers to hear them pitch premises for future episodes. Then our supervising producer and I have a directors meeting where we punch up the latest script with extra gags or try to condense some scenes if it feels a little long. Next, we kick off the board artist with our notes and I usually provide some preliminary drawings for new locations or characters. Second cup of coffee. We usually have network pitch, then we stay for notes from our network producers. I then run into the editor's room to get a nice cleaned cut episode over to the producers for approval. Lunch break! I usually grab something from our fancy Nick café, then lose a few video game matches with Jonathan Rodrigues (character designer on *The Casagrandes*). He's the champ. After being pummeled, I go over sketches with the art director, Miguel Gonzalez to approve for the clean-up stage. Third cup of coffee. I pop in to see how the voice records are going with our cast and usually sneak a few snacks they have for our cast. They get the best snacks…I rush back to breakdown an episode, we call out how many new designs we are going to need for characters, props and backgrounds. Fourth cup of coffee. I read some more premises for pitches, jump on storyboard notes to kick off to my revisionist, check in with my crew to see how their day went, gather all of my Papercutz comics to give them a kiss goodnight and run home because of all the coffee I drank.

What's the biggest difference between writing/storyboarding for animation and comics?

The biggest difference is you have to be more precise when doing comics. In animation, as a board artist myself, I usually draw loose drawings with a few lines dropped in for the backgrounds. You have to be a lot more aware of composition in comics. Same goes with animation, but the characters are going to be moving so you can focus on posing and acting.

Who is your favorite Casagrandes character to work on? Least?

I don't have a least favorite. They are all my favs, but if I had to pick, it's Sergio. He's the punching bag of our show.

We can really go wacky when it comes to him getting hurt.

What's the hardest part of working on cartoons?

Waiting almost a year for our episodes to air. One of our episodes takes about nine months for completion. As you are reading this, we are pitching a show that will be on air in nine months.

Have you ever had writer's block? If so, how did you overcome it?

Everyday. That's why I like to do warm up drawings. I never show those drawings to anybody. I just doodle on a piece of paper, post it note or script. Just to help get the artist block wiggles out.

What advice do you have for kids who want to work in cartoons?

Keep drawing. Carry a sketchbook with you everywhere you go. I have a few laying around in my house. I have one in my car in case I get inspired by something I see. You don't have to show it to anyone, just keep drawing and try out different styles. Learn from those that figured out all the kinks. Learn from comics, animated features, museums, even draw over newspapers by sketching the photos with a pen. That's what I did.

With today's technology, you have a whole animation studio at your fingertips. Learn the programs and be adaptable. Experiment with different styles. Every show is different, so you will not always be drawing in the same style. Keep drawing and have fun.

Do you have a favorite line or gag that got cut out?

Yes, I pitched a gag that made it to the network pitch where Rosa, is holding Sergio like a baby and she takes a giant spoon full of food and she chews it then feeds him like a baby bird by regurgitating into his mouth. It got a ton of laughs but it also grossed out a lot of people. I won't say who, but his name rhymes with Malo Alcatraz.

What's your favorite Casagrandes contribution that you provided?

The saliva in your belly button if you have a stomachache. My mom and my grandmother taught us that remedy and I am telling you all, IT WORKS!

How long does it take to do a storyboard? How long to storyboard an entire episode?

For our show, it takes about seven weeks plus. On week one, we call it the 'PREP' week. This is where the board artists gather all the materials they will need for their episode, like backgrounds, props, characters that are all going to be re-used. This week also includes thumbnail stage for the board artists where they map out the episode with quick little sketches to get an idea to plan out their shot. Then they get three weeks to rough it all out. They pitch us their roughs, make sure it all flows and works. We usually punch it up here with some more gags or dialogue tweaks. Then they have the rest of the three weeks to clean up. At the end of week six, they pitch to the network and our entire crew is there to watch. It's a lot of fun and rewarding to hear the entire room burst into laughter.

LALO ALCARAZ
Consulting Producer/ Cultural Consultant

Where were you born?

I was born in San Diego, California, and I grew up going back and forth across the US/Mexican border.

Was it a large family?

Nope, I was an only child, but I have half-siblings in Mexico. My immediate family was small, but I had friends with big Mexican families. There was always lots of delicious food! I liked being an only child, it probably made me the appealingly self-centered artist I am today.

In what ways was your family similar to the Casagrandes?

We briefly had a parrot. And we had lots of Mexican food, which we just called "food."

In what ways were they different?

My multi-generational family was spread out throughout space and time. (ie. Mexico, and long ago).

What were your interests growing up?
I liked to watch all the TV sitcoms I could, and I loved watching Mexican *lucha libre* movies and drawing comics.

What were your favorite cartoons?

I watched the original *Looney Tunes* and learned all about US pop culture of the 40s. I also enjoyed *Fat Albert* and all the lesser Saturday Morning cartoons.

Who are your greatest influences? Which cartoons and/or animators inspired you most?

My cartooning influence was Gus Arriola, the comic strip artist behind *Gordo*, the first nationally syndicated comic strip by a Mexican-American, or any Latino for that matter. I also enjoyed Mexican comicbooks from Mexico, and later *Doonesbury* and *Bloom County*, which are straight up political comic strips that also made me realize I could use comics to tell lots of stories.

What's your average workday like?

I have five jobs, but I mostly sit in the Casagrandes Writers Room to chime in on jokes and lines, pitch gags, or sometimes check a Spanish word translation.

What's the biggest difference between writing/storyboarding for animation and comics?

The stakes are a lot bigger in animation, and there are so many other people who help create the final product. In comics it can just be you, so you are wholly responsible for the content.

Who is your favorite Casagrandes character to work on? Least?

My favorite character is probably *Abuelo* Hector. My least favorite character is *Abuelo* Hector, because he reminds me of myself a little too much!

What's the hardest part of working on cartoons?

It's hard to watch a perfectly amazing joke get demolished and chucked out the window.

Have you ever had writer's block? If so, how did you overcome it?

I never have writer's block. I have no problem writing bad ideas.

What advice do you have for kids who want to work in cartoons?

Kep on drawing! And never stop!

Do you have a favorite line or gag that got cut out?

Oh, gosh, I have one that Miguel Puga thought was hilarious but that I was eager to cut. You'll have to ask him! It involved vomit.

What's your favorite Casagrandes contribution that you provided?

Well, they named Lalo the dog after me even before the show existed, so that's kind of bragworthy.

IZABELLA ALVAREZ
Voice Actress of Ronnie Anne

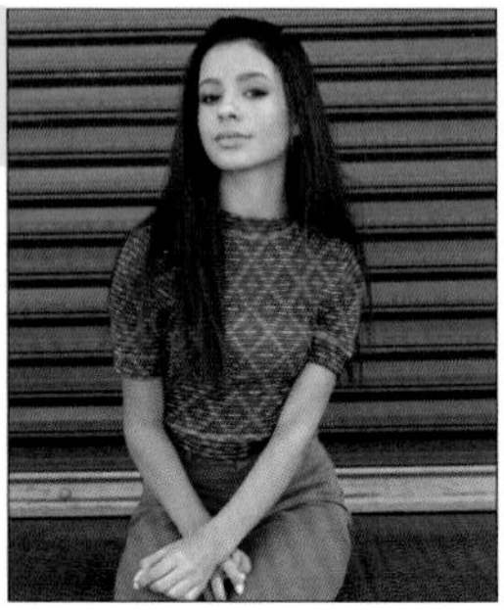

Where/when were you born?

Orange County, California in 2004

What were your interests growing up?

Music. I'm in love with music. I would jam out with my brother growing up and it's gotten me through so so much.

What were you favorite cartoons?

Phineas and Ferb, SpongeBob SquarePants, Tom and Jerry was my jam. *Looney Tunes.*

How did you decide to become a voice actor?

I never had any intention on becoming a voice actor. I had only known live-action my entire life, but growing up everyone would tell me you have to do voiceovers because your voice is so raspy. I always brushed it off until The Casagrandes came around and it was just a perfect fit.

Did you do impressions when you were younger?

Honestly, no, but growing up my brother would do TONS of impressions like Kermit the Frog and Nacho from *Nacho Libre*. I was always around the crazy, funny impressions that he would do.

How did you keep the voices you create consistent?

I honestly don't do much to keep it consistent. It's become so easy for me to snap into Ronnie Anne's voice that it's basically just second nature to me. I can snap into the voice in 2 seconds and keep talking in it for the rest of the day.

What advice do you have for kids who want to become voice actors?

DO IT AND COMMIT. Always commit when you perform especially for voiceover. GO ALL OUT!

What's been your favorite episode so far?

An episode that isn't out yet. ;))) Stay tuned. It's a good one.

Extra-special thanks to Miguel, Izabella, and Lalo (Thanks to Neil Wade for facilitating)! Have more burning questions for the cast and crew of THE CASAGRANDES? E-mail Whitman@papercutz.com with your questions and they could be answered in a future volume!